ESCAPE TO HAPPY EVER AFTER

S J CRABB

♥

Copyrighted Material

Copyright © S J Crabb 2021

S J Crabb has asserted her rights under the Copyright, Designs and Patents Act 1988 to be identified as the Author of this work.

This book is a work of fiction and except in the case of historical fact, any resemblance to actual persons, living or dead, is purely coincidental.
All rights reserved. No part of this book may be reproduced or transmitted in any form without written permission of the author, except by a reviewer who may quote brief passages for review purposes only.

NB: This book uses UK spelling & grammar

ALSO BY S J CRABB

♥

The Diary of Madison Brown

My Perfect Life at Cornish Cottage

My Christmas Boyfriend

Jetsetters

More from Life

A Special Kind of Advent

Fooling in love

Will You

Holly Island

Aunt Daisy's Letter

The Wedding at the Castle of Dreams

My Christmas Romance

Escape to Happy Ever After

sjcrabb.com

ESCAPE TO HAPPY EVER AFTER

Escape to Happy Ever After where all your happy endings are guaranteed.

When Susie Mahoney was gifted a break to Happy Ever After, she couldn't pack her bags quickly enough because she had to do something to break the run of bad luck she was experiencing.

She was fast approaching the age where all her friends had settled down and found their 'one' and she was running out of options.

Happy Ever After, as it turns out, is a sweet little bed & breakfast on the Dorset coast and as soon as she sets eyes on the little cottage nestling in a valley before a sparkling sea, she falls in love.

Surely this is the perfect place to set her life back on track and consider her options. Long walks in the fresh air to concentrate her mind. Hearty meals to raise her energy levels and cosy evenings in the local pub beside a flickering fire curled up with a good book. Perfect.

However, what she didn't realise was the invitation was for two and her 'plus one' was already unpacked and making himself at home. There is also a fossil club convention in town meaning every room on the Jurassic coast is occupied and she has to spend the next week with a stranger.

Freddie Carlton receives an invitation to escape to Happy Ever After and was particularly interested in the 'happy ending' it promised. Having had a disastrous run of bad luck with women he was prepared to try anything.

He wasn't prepared to discover that his 'one' had already been chosen for him and was seriously annoying. A woman who arrived with more baggage than an Airbus and was in no mood to share.

Will Happy Ever After work its magic and give them both the happy ending they deserve, or will fate continue to throw obstacles in their path and turn their bad start into a very complicated ending?

laughing at me. Why wasn't I born a lamb? Life would be so much simpler, and I wouldn't have to deal with LIFE!

Deciding to exit the vehicle as protocol usually dictates, I stare at mini moo in frustration. Why? Why now? You've always been so reliable, so solid. Why now when I'm miles from anywhere with only a lamb for company?

The thought of locating the problem myself doesn't even occur to me. I'm not a mechanic, why would I know? I can't even google my way out of this because apparently those undulating hills serve to keep the rest of the world out and there's no signal!

The fact I'm blocking the road is also a bit of a problem. I say road, more like a track, and I stare around me nervously in case a car decides to finish the job and put mini moo out of her misery.

Feeling frustrated, I wonder if I can walk to a neighbouring farmhouse where a friendly farmer's wife will welcome me in and pour me a mug of tea from her ever boiling pot on the Aga and cut me a slice of homemade apple cake. Yes, that's a good idea. She will have a land line and happily offer to help me and I can wait in her farmhouse kitchen and warm my toes in front of her fire in the rocking chair. Yes, that's going to happen, I just know it.

However, all around me are just fields, lambs and a now oppressive silence.

Taking a deep breath, I climb back into my car and try to turn the ignition. It just makes that whirring sound that tells me it's not happy and isn't going anywhere. The phone signal doesn't even have one bar and I feel like crying. What now?

It's taken me several hours to get this far, and Happy Ever After must be only ten minutes away.

It will be dark soon, and what if no one comes? Maybe a murderer will the first one on the scene and they will find my car and I'll be missing presumed dead. I expect that's going to happen because it's just my luck.

Resting my head against the steering wheel, I squeeze my eyes tightly shut. Why me, why is it always me? Why can't I go anywhere, or do anything without something bad happening?

Suddenly, I hear a sound – of life and look up with hope flaring in my heart. I'm being rescued. This is it; someone will save me and he will be a billionaire on his way to his mansion. He will stop and fall in love with me on the spot, and all my troubles will vanish like smoke on a windy day. He will be tall, dark and handsome and look a little like Tom Cruise in his glory days although much taller. Actually, scrub that, he will be Chris Hemsworth dressed as Thor wielding his sword.

So, it's with a little disappointment that I see a tractor heading towards me and my heart sinks even more as he sounds some kind of horn thing and waves at me to move aside. Once again, I exit the car and stand waving apologetically, mouthing, "Help me."

The man inside looks irritable and rolls his eyes and squeals to a halt and jumps down from his monster vehicle. As he saunters towards me, yet again my heart sinks when I see he is no Chris Hemsworth, or Liam come to mention it. He is angry!

"You can't park there."

"I'm not parked, I've broken down."

"You can't break down here either."

"Tell that to my car."

"Listen lady, I have a herd of cows heading this way and your car had better not be in their way."

Looking over my shoulder in horror, I picture them stampeding mini moo and it's not a pleasant image.

"Can you help me?" My voice sounds rather high and

damsel in distressy and he blows out – hard.

"I'm not the emergency services love."

"But you're all I've got until I can get a phone signal to call them."

"What's the matter with it then?"

"I don't know, she just stopped."

"She?"

He raises a sarcastic eye, yes, there is such a thing and blows out again, I would say exhale but this man doesn't do anything by halves and I'm guessing he doesn't meet many people because his art of conversation is seriously off.

"Yes, mini moo is a she and *she* has let me down badly."

"Mini what?"

"Moo, like in the cows that are heading our way as we speak. Please help me, you're my only hope."

I think he whispers something like, "Bloody grockle," and I wonder if this a Dorsetonian swear word. I really must look it up when I reach the land of google but for now, I am completely at his mercy.

Remembering my manners, I say formally, "I'm pleased to meet you, I'm Susie Mahoney and I…"

He kicks the tyre and I say in outrage, "Excuse me, what are you doing?"

"Checking for a flat."

"Oh, that's alright then, I mean, having eyes isn't enough around here is it? I mean, a good old kick will really tell you what your eyes can't."

He shrugs and runs his fingers through his hair, and I notice a tattoo of a lamb on his bicep. Come to think of it, this man's arms are a walking farmyard because he has every farm animal going tattooed on his arm, with names too.

I stare at him with interest as he grumbles, "I'll get my brother to drag it out with his landrover."

"Drag it! Can't you just call the AA man? I mean, they do

have actual ways of making cars roadworthy again and I'm sure dragging it will do more harm than good."

"Don't have time, the cows."

He turns away and grabs some kind of walkie talkie thing from his tractor and speaks into it with words I don't recognise. Grockle, airhead and townie are littered with expletives and carry towards my ears on the bleat of a lamb's cry.

He returns and says gruffly, "He's on his way."

He turns to leave and I say slightly hysterically, "Where are you going?"

"Got work to do."

He heaves his body back into the tractor and the engine noise drowns out my plea to stay with me. I watch in disbelief as he reverses his tractor back up the road, and then I see him enter the lamb's field. As he passes me on the other side of the hedge, he shouts, "I'll head off the cows."

He goes before I can answer, leaving me stranded once again with just the promise of a landrover and his brother to rescue me. Hoping against hope his brother is some kind of hot body building, billionaire farmer, I sit down and wait for the love god to arrive.

CHAPTER 2

It's doubtful there are any billionaires in Dorset, or Hemsworths, although there appears to be plenty of Thors, minus the good looks and personality. The brother of the previous ungallant knight arrives, looking even more irritated as he wordlessly hooks up mini moo to the tow bar and says roughly, "Get in, you'll have to steer."

"What?"

He rolls his eyes and growls, "I'll tow you, just keep the car level with mine, handbrake off, can you manage that?"

"Of course, I can drive, you know."

He doesn't even reply and just turns and jumps into probably the oldest landrover in existence and the noise of the engine mocks me because how on earth is that death trap still functioning, while my mini moo is broken - much like its owner?

Somehow, I manage to keep my car level and allow myself to be pulled down the track behind the angry man.

It takes about ten minutes before he pulls off the road, then heads up another track that leads into a courtyard where there are several industrial barns filled with decaying farm machinery and bales of hay.

I watch as he exits his car that should be illegal and heads across. "Where are you heading?"

"Happy ever after."

A faint smile ghosts his lips and he nods, seemingly unfazed by my reply.

"I'll give you a ride, you can arrange to collect your car from there."

"Wait, you want me to leave mini moo here?"

"Mini what?"

He starts to laugh and I say defensively, "My car, we've been through a lot together and she deserves some respect."

Shaking his head, he says roughly, "Grab any valuables, it's not far, Kevin will sort your car out."

"Who's Kevin?"

"Owns the place you're going. A bit strange, but nice enough."

Goodness, if he thinks Kevin's strange, he must be certifiable because the 'shame they're not the Hemsworth brothers' are the strangest men I think I've ever met.

Grabbing my handbag and keeping a tight grip on my phone, I surreptitiously snap a photo of his number plate and send it to Polly. You can't be too careful and if this man is a murderer, at least my forward thinking will bring him to justice.

As I open the door of the rusty old landrover, I gag a little. It smells like a farmyard in here and looks as if the pigs live in here at night. The seat is missing most of the padding that oozes out of the ripped fabric and makes me shiver inside. The mud on the mats is old and caked on and there's a slight pungent odour that makes me long for the days of face masks once again.

There doesn't even appear to be any comforts in this

contraption, calling it a car would be against the trade descriptions act and so I perch on the edge of the seat and note with a sinking feeling that there's not even a seatbelt.

It's not even legal and I could very much end my life on this journey and if that happens, I am so haunting the hell out of this man and his brother.

We set off and bone-shaker isn't even close. I think I hit the roof several times as any suspension this car/death trap ever had, is long gone. The window appears to be stuck on open and there's a cool breeze coming from the air vent along with the toxic smell of burning diesel.

Thor number 2 doesn't even try to make conversation and neither do I because I couldn't hear him if he shouted with a megaphone. My ears are ringing, my nerves are jangling, and I'm a physical and emotional wreck as we pull into the driveway of a place called Happy Ever After.

This is more like it.

The little thatched cottage that nestles at the end of the driveway looks warm and welcoming with its newly thatched roof. Tulips are lining the route and the sun beams its welcome through the fruit trees, holding their blossom with pride.

The sea sparkles in the distance, and a feeling of pure calm washes over me. Polly was right. This place is just what the doctor prescribed because some of the tension leaves me immediately.

Farmer Thor grinds to a halt and says roughly, "Here you go. They'll sort you out but don't leave your car up at the farm long, if it's in our way, we'll drag it to the side."

"Um, of course, thank you. Um, how much do I owe you?"

"For what?"

"The ride."

"Nothing, just get the car off our land."

"Of course, quick as I can."

I exit the car like a bat out of hell and he doesn't hang around and churns up the gravel as he leaves the way we came.

For some strange inexplicable reason, my eyes fill with tears and I feel so alone. I'm stranded in the middle of nowhere in a strange place and my belongings are somewhere hostile, living in fear of being dragged around by a mechanical beast, operated by a human one.

Suddenly, I hear a friendly voice, "Welcome to Happy Ever After, you must be Susie."

Turning around, I look with interest at the beaming woman who is heading my way.

Her arms are out as if she's greeting a long-lost relative and I shuffle on my feet, feeling suddenly nervous.

"Um, hi..."

"Sandra dear, Sandra Anderson. Proprietor of Happy Ever After, where all your happy endings are guaranteed."

"Oh, I'm pleased to meet you."

She actually does envelop me in a hug and then steps back and looks me over. "You need fattening up, a decent night's sleep, and possibly a relaxing bath with essential oils. Leave it with me, my dear, you'll soon be back to your usual self in no time."

"Sounds good."

I'm not lying, it does. This is heaven. Sandra is obviously an angel sent from God because she has ticked all my boxes in one sentence. She takes my hand and leads me towards her pretty cottage, and I briefly wonder if this is what Hansel and Gretel experienced before they were abducted by the wicked witch.

However, Sandra is no wicked witch because hallelujah, I

spy a kettle whistling on the Aga and the heavenly scent of freshly baked bread hits me as soon as we venture inside.

"Now dear, take a seat and I'll fix you a cup of tea and a snack; I'm guessing you must be hungry."

As she turns away, I take the seat gratefully, and she says with interest, "I didn't see your car, or your luggage."

"Oh yes, there's a bit of a story there."

I fill her in and she shakes her head. "You poor thing, what a terrible thing to happen. No worries, it sounds as if you came across the Armstrongs. They're a little blustery but are kind enough and your car will be perfectly safe with them. I'll get Kevin to take you back there after dinner tonight, I'm guessing you'll only be happy when you've got your stuff."

She hands me a steaming mug of tea and pushes a bowl of sugar and a small jug of milk towards me.

"Here, help yourself and I'll make you a nice ham sandwich, you're not a vegetarian, are you?"

"No, that sounds good, you are very kind."

"Not at all, now eat up, I'll run and get Kevin."

She leaves me to relax in what must surely be heaven and I laugh as an inquisitive nose pushes a door open at the far side and looks at me through large brown doe eyes.

"Hey there, what's your name?"

The little dog comes bounding in and jumps on my lap, and I laugh as he licks my face. "You are so sweet, what's your name little one? Maybe we'll be best friends, I could sure use one right now."

He licks me again and I laugh and stroke him, feeling instantly better about life. Yes, this place is amazing and I am looking forward to the perfect getaway.

CHAPTER 3

Sandra soon returns with the mysterious Kevin, who looks normal enough. He beams and shakes my hand before growling, "Timmy, on your bed."

The little dog scoots off my lap and jumps into his bed by the Aga and wags his tail. "He's so adorable."

Sandra laughs. "He's a scamp, you'll have to be firm with him or he'll latch onto you like a leech if he gets his way and you won't be rid of him."

I shrug, "It's fine; I love dogs, I'm not so good with cats but dogs, that's different."

Kevin takes a seat across from me and accepts a steaming mug of tea gratefully.

"Interesting that your car broke down, is that normal?"

"No, she's usually so reliable. I mean, I've been a member of the AA for years and never had to use them. It just sort of stopped at the most inconvenient moment."

Kevin looks thoughtful. "Can I ask if you have any enemies?"

"Excuse me?"

I stare at him in shock and Sandra says quickly, "Enough,

Kevin, of course someone like Susie doesn't have any enemies."

"Do you?"

Kevin looks at me with interest and I say nervously, "I don't think so, why?"

He leans back and takes a sip of his drink and then says thoughtfully, "An ex-boyfriend that you dumped, a woman scorned perhaps, maybe a stalker - that could work."

"No, um, nothing like that, except… actually you're right. Oh my god, you *are* right, all of the above. What are you thinking?"

He looks at his wife triumphantly, causing her to roll her eyes.

"Perhaps they cut the brakes, fiddled with the fuel, slashed the tyres, it's not uncommon when a person's out to commit…"

"Kevin!"

Sandra looks at me apologetically. "Take no notice of him, Susie, you'll soon get used to Kevin. Anyway, let me show you to your room, I'm sure you're in need of a freshen up."

I follow her out, feeling a little out of sorts. What is this place and who are these people? It's as if I stumbled from Hell into the twilight zone.

Sandra laughs softly as we head outside and walk down a path surrounded by tulips and hyacinths. The scent is powerful and does a good job of calming my jangled nerves, and Sandra laughs softly. "Don't mind Kevin, he's a little inventive with reality. Just ignore him, I do most of the time, it keeps me sane."

I note with interest the row of doors set in what appears to be a converted stable block. They look newly refurbished and there must be at least five rooms here. She stops outside the middle one and says brightly, "Here we are, number 3. You should find a few personal items inside if you want that bath we spoke of but I'm guessing your companion will have some you can use. Dinner is at 6pm and Kevin will take you to get your car as soon as you've finished."

She heads off and as I turn to go inside, her words hit me like a violent hailstorm. Companion?

"Excuse me?"

Quickly, I race back to her and say loudly, "Um, sorry Sandra, did you say companion?"

She turns and looks at me in surprise. "Yes, Mr Carlton. I must say, he's a lovely man and is very handsome, you're a lucky girl."

"Mr Carlton, what, Miles?"

I stare at her in shock because why would Polly's boyfriend Miles be here?"

Sandra looks confused. "I don't think he was called Miles, I'm sure his name is Freddie."

"Freddie? I'm sorry, Sandra, but I booked a single room, I don't know who he is."

Sandra looks worried. "Oh dear, I'm sorry, but the booking was very specific. Mr Freddie Carlton and Miss Susie Mahoney. I never make a mistake. Are you saying that you don't know this man?"

"Yes."

"I stare at her in shock and she shakes her head, looking worried. "Maybe you should check with your friend who made the booking. Miss Proudlock, I believe. I wouldn't forget such an unusual name."

She makes to leave and I grab her arm, "Please, can you give me another room, I don't care where, just…I can't…share."

I think I'm almost hyperventilating and she looks sympathetic. "I'm so sorry. There aren't any more rooms. You've picked one of the busiest weekends of the year. The Lyme Bay fossil convention is in town, and every room is taken as far as Exeter and Bournemouth. If your friend hadn't booked so early, you wouldn't have got a room for miles. I can always arrange a cot bed if you like. I'm sure I have a spare one knocking around here somewhere."

"A cot bed! No, I need a room, my own space, anything. A caravan, a tent even, it's just that I can't share with a …stranger."

Sandra pats my arm sympathetically. "Maybe see how it goes for tonight and as soon as your car is on the mend, you can decide whether to stay, or go. It will be fine, like I said he's a really nice guy, I can think of worse people to be stranded with."

She winks and sets off, leaving me standing there looking after her riddled with anxiety.

Grabbing my phone, I almost howl in frustration when I see no signal in sight and feel like smashing it on the ground under the heel of my shoe. Bloody Polly and Miles, what are they playing at arranging this getaway with a stranger? Freddie Carlton must be Miles's brother. What on earth were they thinking?

CHAPTER 4

My heart thumps and I know just how a cat burglar must feel as I venture into the room and shout, "Is anybody here?"

I note the pretty room that I would ordinarily be so excited to discover. A huge brass bed covered in crisp white sheets, with pretty scatter cushions positioned perfectly. Soft beige carpeting and pretty wooden painted furniture holding lamps and a vase of flowers. A lovely picture of the scenery outside hangs on the wall and white curtains billow at the open window, restoring peace to a crazy world I happened upon.

"Um, hello."

I call out again because it's obvious that someone is here already, given away by the bag slung on the chair in the corner and the sound of a shower running through a door to the side.

Swallowing nervously, I wonder if I should leave because this man may pop out at any moment in nothing but a towel, fingers crossed, anyway.

The shower stops and I try again, "Um, hello, Mr Carlton."

The sound of the door handle turning makes me take a step back and my mouth drops as the man himself heads into the room dressed in nothing but a curious smile and a small towel fixed around his waist.

"Can I help you?"

I can't speak. Words no longer exist in my brain because I can only look. From the wet, tousled hair that he is raking his fingers through. The curious blue eyes that stare at my soul and rip it from me in a haze of lust. The rippling muscles of biceps that could wrestle a bear and a whole stadium of Thors and the bare chest that glistens with water that makes me take an involuntary step towards it.

My eyes lower and I swallow hard as I see the strong legs of a man who looks as if fitness is his passion and I can't tear my eyes from the floor as he repeats, "I'm sorry, can I help you?"

"Um, Freddie Carlton, I presume."

"Yes." He shifts a little and says irritably, "Look, I'm sorry but could you get on with it, it's just that I'm freezing my nuts off because the door is wide open."

"Oh, of course, I'm sorry."

Averting my eyes, I turn and close the door and he says roughly, "I'm sorry, am I missing something, it's just I wasn't expecting company?"

Shaking myself, I fix my gaze on the wall behind him and say firmly, "Look, don't freak out or anything, but we appear to both be booked into this room. I know, mad isn't it?" I laugh nervously. "Anyway, you can blame your brother and Polly for that because they obviously thought it would be hilarious to meddle in our lives. Well, to cut a long story short, there are no more rooms for miles around and my car is out of action presumed dead. So, if you like, I'll help you pack and you can return home and tell your brother exactly what you think of him."

I take a deep breath and close my eyes tightly shut. There, I've done it and told him where we stand. If I feel bad that he must leave, I can't worry about it because it was not my mistake.

"I'm not leaving."

I open one eye. "What?"

He folds his arms across that woman magnet chest and says bluntly, "What's the problem?"

I just stare in amazement. "The problem is, we are strangers. There are no other rooms and we are expected to, um, cohabit here this week. Well, I'm sorry to break it to you, but I'm not that kind of girl and I have standards, high ones, actually. So, if you were a true gentleman, you would recognise that I have no other choice and that you, as the only one of us who has a working vehicle, will do the decent thing and leave."

"Who said I was a gentleman? I've been looking forward to this trip and I'm *not* leaving. It's taken me the best part of a day to get here and the only thing I'm doing is drying off, changing and then heading out to find the local pub. You can join me if you like and you may find I'm not that bad and we can make the best of a bad situation. Your choice."

"But…"

He stares at me with a challenge in his eyes and I feel myself blushing as my traitorous gaze heads lower, hating myself for wondering what he's hiding underneath that towel.

"Listen, babe, let me get some clothes on and we'll grab a drink somewhere. I suppose it is kind of funny when you think about it. I'm guessing you must be a friend of Polly's. Just wait until I get back, I'll think of a way to pay them back for this. You have to admit, as pranks go, it's a good one."

"A prank, are you kidding me?"

"Chill out, my family is always doing stuff like this. I'm used to it, which is why I'm probably not as hysterical as you are."

"You think I'm hysterical?" I hate the way my voice races an octave and he laughs softly. "Yes, I do. Anyway, as I said, I'm freezing my nuts off here, so if you don't mind."

He leans across and grabs something from his bag and actually winks at me before heading back the way he came.

I think my mouth hits the floor as I watch him go because God have mercy on my soul, I'm interested.

Two hours later and I am no longer interested. It didn't take me long to realise that Freddie Carlton is extremely bad for my health. If I could, I'd have an inoculation against him because given half a chance, he would ruin me.

Against my better judgement, I went with him to the local pub and despite the fact I could actually live here, it's becoming increasingly obvious I couldn't live with him. As soon as we stepped foot inside the door, he went on some kind of charm offensive that resulted in us being seated at the best table overlooking the sea, and the waitress couldn't do enough for us – him. I watched as he flirted his way to a couple of beers, some bar snacks and a potted history of the area, all the while adding another member to his fan club.

After a while, I decide that I'm the third wheel and stare at the woman who appears to have forgotten she's here to do a job and not to flirt with the clientele. "Listen, I'm sorry, but could you give us a minute, we really need to talk."

The waitress – Kimberly throws me a look that could curdle milk and tosses back her chestnut gleaming hair that is straight out of a Loreal commercial.

"Sure."

She looks at Freddie and smiles seductively. "You know where to find me."

As she flounces off, Freddie leans forward and whispers, "Thanks for that, I thought she'd never go."

"Are you kidding me, she only stayed because you encouraged her?"

"I did not."

"Yes, you did. You flirted shamelessly with her, and she couldn't believe her luck. I'm sure if she could, she would have shoved me aside and taken my place and I would have ended up doing her work."

I drum my fingers irritably on the table and he leans back and smirks. "Jealous?"

"Of her, you're delusional."

"I can tell you are."

"I'm not, you flatter yourself."

"I glare at him and he laughs softly. "I like you, Susie, you're hilarious."

Did I miss something here because I am feeling anything but hilarious? Suddenly, it strikes me that the reason Freddie is still single is probably because he's not all there – mentally speaking. I mean, physically speaking, he appears to be all there with bells on. I don't think I have ever met such an attractive man and Sandra was right, I am a lucky girl to be shacked up with him but really, he is not quite all the ticket.

"What?"

"What do you mean, what?" I stare at him in confusion and he laughs. "You look as if you're chewing a wasp. What's up?"

"Listen, um, Freddie. You seem like a nice guy, a little too nice really given the fact the waitress obviously wants to put you on a leash and tether you to her side for posterity. However, this isn't going to work. I mean, I came here for a week of rest and recuperation because quite frankly, I have had a bad man year, actually a bad man decade and having to share my week of contemplation with a man like you, well, it may impede my recovery."

"I'm a good listener, maybe I can help."

"No, I'm not ready to talk about the one hundred reasons why I'm sworn off men for good."

He leans forward and my breath hitches because those blue eyes are now directed on me and it's a lot to deal with. "You're not the only one."

"What?"

"With issues."

I knew it. I wonder what his are because I could die happy with his issues and I watch fascinated as he shakes his head sadly. "To be honest, I get it, I really do. I'm a bit of a loser when it comes to women."

I snort and then cover my mouth with my hand as he raises his eyes and smirks. Laughing, he leans back and takes a sip of his beer and then sighs. "The thing is, I'm a bit of a mess, emotionally speaking. Miles and Polly probably sent me here as a last resort because it appears that I have terrible taste in women."

I lean forward and say with interest. "I'm a good listener."

We share a smile and he laughs softly. "You see, I've had a disastrous run of relationships that usually end badly. I appear attracted to women with looks but no personality. The only thing we have in common is sex, and that gets boring over time when you don't actually like the person. Then I go through a messy break up and am on to the next shallow, empty headed woman with no morals, or manners. So, you see, I'm a bad judge of character and rather than sectioning me for my own safety, I suppose they have sent me here to save me from myself."

Thinking of the barmaid, I shake my head. "I can see why,

I mean, five minutes in and you already have one potential candidate lined up."

I look at the barmaid who is throwing death stares my way.

Freddie sighs. "I can't help myself, I'm over friendly. I know that and women seem to take it the wrong way. They take my openness as a sign of attraction. What would you do?"

"You're asking me, the woman who gets it wrong every time. Over and over again, making the same mistakes and not learning from them. Maybe you're right and Polly did this for my own good. Perhaps we are each other's therapy dogs and should cold turkey together."

He laughs and throws that hussy making stare my way, and I think a little piece of my heart jumps across the table to join his. "Then let's just enjoy the week, chill out, cohabit, as you put it, with no strings attached. Maybe we can work out where we're going wrong and leave this place with a fool proof plan leading to happiness."

"Sounds good to me."

I raise my glass to his and as they touch, we stare at each other and smile. "To therapy dogs and our future happiness."

He grins. "To therapy dogs and our happy ever after."

I smile as I take a swig of my drink that I'm wondering if the barmaid poisoned and then lean back in my chair. Yes, maybe this could work. Friends, that what I need, no emotion and no worries.

CHAPTER 5

*D*inner is a strange affair. As soon as we returned, we went straight to the dining room to enjoy some kind of feast laid on by our welcoming hosts.

We are not the only ones.

As we sit at a table for two by the window, I look around with interest.

There is a table of six men in the centre of the room and they seem like average guys. From their conversation, they are here for the convention and by the looks of them, they all need a woman in their lives and fast. Zero fashion sense and an awkwardness that tells me they are more at home with relics than the living, and Freddie looks like a movie star compared to them.

Next to their table is a couple who look a little older than us. They spend most of the time on their phones, but I see the woman stealing looks at Freddie and then looking away hurriedly. He doesn't appear to notice and just eats his food as if he's never had an actual meal before and can't eat fast enough, and the man with the woman is oblivious to everything.

The room feels crowded because it's a little cottage and probably wasn't designed for mass entertaining, and we whisper because every word we say can be heard by the other diners.

"You should try the pie, it's amazing."

Freddie offers me a forkful of his beer and ale pie, and I lean forward without thinking and groan as he feeds me. "Hmmm."

He nods, "I told you it was good. Do you think they allow residential borders, I could relocate here?"

"What do you do, for a living, I mean?"

"I'm an architect."

"Really."

"You sound shocked."

"I suppose I am."

"What did you think I did?"

Images of the dream boys and male strippers crowd my mind and I laugh softly.

"What's so funny?"

"Nothing."

"Then why are you laughing?"

"No reason."

"Yes, there is. Why is me being an architect funny?"

"I don't know, I suppose it doesn't really suit you. I mean, don't take this the wrong way, but you don't look the type."

"What is the type?"

I lean forward and whisper. "There are six of them not far away. I wouldn't bat an eyelid if you told me they were architects but you, no way."

"So, what did you think I was?"

"A stripper."

He laughs out loud and everyone in the room looks at us, which makes me giggle and he smiles.

"That's better."

"What is?"

"Seeing you smile. I was wondering if you had it in you."

"I can smile, why, I'm not that serious, am I?"

"You kind of are."

Sighing, I spear another piece of his pie and grin wickedly.

"Like I said, I don't have much to smile about."

"Do you want to tell me about it?"

"Not really, it will just make you pity me, maybe hate me a little and decide I'm the type of girl who deserves everything she got."

"I doubt that."

He spears a piece of my quiche and grins. "I like eating your food, it's so much better than eating mine, it feels forbidden."

"I agree."

I pinch another piece of his pie and we grin, sharing a look that immediately has me building walls quickly inside. Oh no, this isn't happening. He is not wearing down my defences so easily, I mean a pie for goodness' sake, my kingdom for a pie, not happening.

Leaning back, I look around me with interest and try to distance myself from this strange relationship that's forming.

"This place is lovely, so warm and welcoming."

"It is."

He pushes his plate away and says with interest. "So, tell me, Susie, what do *you* do? I've told you, now it's your turn."

I can feel the heat tearing through me as I stutter, "Um, nothing interesting."

"Go on, it must be way more interesting than being an architect. You nearly yawned when I told you, so whatever it is you do must be super exciting."

"Not really." I take a gulp of wine and wonder if I should lie, make something up rather than spill the dreadful truth. Just the thought of the look on his face when he hears what it is, is feeding my anxiety and luckily, I'm spared from answering when Sandra stops by our table and smiles.

"Let me clear your plates away, did you enjoy the meal?"

"Super."

We say it at the same time and stare at each other in surprise as she laughs. "Good, I hope you've left room for treacle sponge and custard."

"Definitely."

Once again, we say the same thing at the same time and I am now really spooked about this. Freddie also looks a little surprised, and Sandra laughs softly.

"Coming right up."

She leaves and we just stare at each other and then I look away, feeling a little out of sorts.

Freddie says quickly, "So, what is it, you never said?"

"It's nothing interesting - really."

"Come on." He laughs. "What's the big secret because from the look on your face, you're embarrassed. I know, you're a circus trapeze act that performs in nothing but a g string and a smile."

He laughs as I look around and whisper furiously, "Trust you to lower the tone."

"Well, what is it, oh I know, you're a belly dancer that performs at intimate gatherings?"

"For goodness' sake, Freddie." I hiss because we now have the attention of the fossil table and even the man next door has looked up from his phone.

Freddie laughs. "Perhaps you're a topless waitress in a gentleman's club."

"Enough, stop. Honestly, your mind is in the gutter, what's wrong with working in a shop, or a bank? Why do you assume that I'd be involved in doing something sleazy or degrading to women?"

"Because you look the type."

I can't form words, and just stare at him in shock and notice out of the corner of my eye that there is now zero conversation in the room. They are trying not to make it obvious, but absolutely everyone is waiting to hear what I say next.

Freddie leans back and winks and a little of my inner devil comes out to play and I say casually, "You're right, I do work in the exotic industry."

You could hear a pin drop as the room stills and I whisper, "I'm, a masseuse at an exclusive club in town." I wink and lower my voice sexily. "I mean, I know you're a stranger and we only just met, but I would be happy to oblige. My services in return for sharing your bed. Who wouldn't be happy about that?"

I hear a sharp intake of breath from the woman beside me and feel the interest of eight pairs of eyes zoning in on me. Leaning back, I cross my legs and say huskily, "So, are you ready for your first session?"

Freddie's eyes glitter with mischief as he plays along.

"How do you want me?"

The tension in the room surrounds us as I lean forward and whisper huskily, "Naked, face down on the bed, I may need to straddle you, is that ok with you?"

From somewhere I think I hear a groan and Freddie nods. "We should leave."

"Yes, we should."

Before we can though, Kevin appears and says loudly, "Hey, Susie, as soon as you've finished, I'll take you to get your car if you like. I have the Kirrin wagon primed and ready to double as an emergency vehicle."

"The Kirrin wagon?" He nods and says in a whisper. "We

used to run Famous Five themed mini breaks. This place was called Kirrin cottage and so we labelled the minivan the Kirrin wagon. It's stuck ever since."

"Why did you change direction?" Freddie looks interested and Kevin sighs. "The books weren't as popular as they were and it lost it's magic, so we re-branded. Everyone wants a happy ever after, so we ran with it. Anyway, the Kirrin wagon stayed and is now at your service."

Looking up, I smile with relief. "You are so kind; I really appreciate it."

Freddie looks surprised. "What's happened?"

"I told you, my car is out of action at some farm in the wilderness. It's got all my luggage in it and I really need my stuff. I can't stay here with nothing, can I?"

"Well…"

"No, I can't." I look at him pointedly and he grins.

"I can take you; I have a car."

"It's fine, I'll do it." Kevin interrupts and we stare up at him in surprise because for some reason we both appear to have forgotten he was here.

"I'll meet you out the front, don't rush and make sure to enjoy Sandra's treacle sponge. I know I do, several times a week actually."

Kevin laughs as he leaves the room and Freddie grins.

"I bet he does."

"Shh, he'll hear you."

Freddie shrugs. "Anyway, I'll help, it will be good to do something to work off all these carbs."

Noting the room is still hanging on our every word, I smirk. "Don't worry, honey, I'll give you a workout you've never experienced in your life before."

From somewhere, something drops on the table and Freddie grins because in one conversation we have elevated ourselves to a scandalous couple who will now be the talk of Happy Ever After.

Mind you, if they knew what I really did to earn my keep, they would probably come to the same conclusion, anyway.

CHAPTER 6

*I*t feels a little strange to be in some kind of van taxi thing, heading through the Dorset countryside to rescue mini moo. Freddie is chatting beside Kevin who is driving and I have the luxury of eight seats in the back.

After the first few minutes, I decide that Kevin is completely mad.

"So, tell me, Freddie, if you came home and found your wife in bed with the gardener, would you throw her out, kill them both in a stabbing frenzy, or join in?"

I catch Freddie's eye in the mirror and hold my breath. To his credit, his voice sounds quite normal as he says firmly, "Throw them out. I mean, the other choices are a little extreme, don't you think?"

"Hmm, maybe."

Once again, I catch his eye and pretend to silently scream which makes him laugh.

"Why do you ask, Kevin?"

"No reason."

I'm not sure why my heart is beating so fast because now

I feel as if I did meet that murderer in Dorset and I thank God Freddie will be his first victim, which might give me time to escape, although the door on this van is seriously heavy and not suitable for a quick getaway.

"So, if that same wife took out an insurance policy on your life and didn't tell you, would you be suspicious and wonder if she plans on killing you?"

Freddie manages to keep his voice even as he says brightly, "I think I'd just ask her. I mean, not everything in life requires a killing spree at the end of it."

"Good point."

Kevin appears thoughtful and then says brightly, "Here we are, Coltdale farm."

We pull into the courtyard and I am relieved to see mini moo exactly where I left her. Glad to have reached her in one piece, I feel quite emotional when I see her waiting.

As Freddie helps me from the minivan, he pulls me close and whispers, "Did you find that conversation seriously weird?"

"What do you think?"

I shake my head and he laughs softly, "He's a character, that's for sure."

Kevin opens the back door of the minivan and says loudly, "We will put your luggage in the back and maybe take a look at the car. It may be something we can repair ourselves, if not, I'll call the AA when we return."

Pulling away from Freddie, I flick the lock on my car and start heaving out my luggage.

Freddie says in astonishment, "How is this possible?"

"What?"

"That all these bags came out of a mini? I mean, how long are you staying for exactly, it looks as if you're moving home?"

He starts to laugh as I say crossly, "Don't overreact, this is nothing."

Kevin nods. "Yes, I saw a woman once with twice this amount. It took her so long to unpack she had to start packing again straight away before her stay ended."

We laugh as Kevin starts loading the minivan and Freddie says incredulously, "I mean, seriously, no wonder the car conked out, it was exhausted."

"Funny, ha, ha." I throw him the keys. "Anyway, why don't you take a look and see if your superior brain can find out why she conked out, as you put it?"

I laugh as Freddie attempts to squash his large body into the car and curses as his knees hit the steering wheel as he struggles to adjust the seat so he can actually fit inside. I start to giggle as he bumps his head and swears and Kevin laughs beside me. "I'm guessing it's not a man's car."

"You could be right."

Once he's inside and probably for life, Freddie attempts to start the car but as it did before, it just makes a weird noise and he shakes his head. "Classic."

"What is?"

Both Kevin and I peer inside and Freddie says loudly, "She's out of petrol and despite what you think, cars don't run on sunshine and rainbows."

He rolls his eyes and I poke my head in and stare at the fuel gauge. "But…"

"Hmm, as I thought, someone probably cut your fuel line. Maybe we should check."

I manage to bump heads with Freddie as I pull out and look at Kevin in surprise. "You think somebody cut my fuel line – deliberately."

Freddie laughs. "As if, no, you just forgot to fill up, like I said, classic."

"It was full when I left home, I must have a leak."

Somehow, Freddie manages to free himself from the car and looks at me incredulously. "Well, cars have a strange habit of using petrol when they move, weird but true. Maybe this car used up all its petrol, and I know this is a shocking thought but maybe it was relying on you to notice and give it some more."

I must admit to feeling a little foolish because mini moo usually lasts a week on a full tank and I suppose I was so lost in my thoughts, I never even thought to check the fuel gauge but I'm not about to admit that, so I say firmly, "I agree with Kevin, somebody obviously cut the line; I should really report this to the police."

"I'll take you if you like."

Kevin interrupts and Freddie surprises me by putting his arm around me and pulling me close, saying firmly, "It's fine. I'll protect you from the murderer, Susie, and first thing tomorrow, take you to the petrol station and buy you a can of petrol to fix the problem. There, no harm done and then we can get on with our trip."

Kevin shakes his head. "No need, I always carry a can of petrol with me, anyway."

Once again, I share a look with Freddie and he raises his eyes as Kevin rummages in the back of the minivan and produces a canister of fuel.

"Here we go, I even have a funnel."

He moves across to my car and I remove the petrol cap gratefully. "I'll pay to replace it, let me know how much I owe you."

"That's fine, I'll add it your bill at the end."

Soon we are ready to leave and despite the fact it's the most uncomfortable car possible for him, Freddie decided to take the journey with me and I can't say I blame him. The less time spent with Hannibal Lecter here, the better. So as Kevin drives off with my luggage, I have a different package to transport and now we are squashed in such a close space, I am feeling a little heady.

Freddie not only fills my personal space physically, but mentally I'm drowning. For some reason, he commands all of my attention. If I'm not inhaling the scent of pure sexual attraction, I'm listening to him speak with an ever-growing fascination. For some reason, I totally understand him. We think along the same lines and I find it easy to relax with him. The trouble is, I know he interests me and it's that thought that bothers me the most because I came here to get away from men like him. I need something else, someone normal, not the drop-dead gorgeous player who will break my heart before moving on to the next one. That's why I must channel my mind and place him firmly in the friend's zone because Freddie Carlton is *not* my happy ever after.

CHAPTER 7

*M*aybe I did pack too much.

I stare around the room in dismay as Freddie brings the last of my cases inside and groans. "That's the last of it, I mean, seriously, do you really need all this?"

"Of course, in case it escaped your attention, we are in England in May. We could experience all types of weather this week. One day it could be so cold I need my ski suit, another day we could be at the beach and I need my bikini and sun hat. I will need wet weather gear and dry weather gear. Three changes of clothes a day and clean underwear with spares just in case."

"In case of what?"

"I don't know, just in case. Then there's the evening wear, the day wear, the jumpers or the t-shirts. Obviously, a change of nightie every night, not to mention the bathrobe because you can't always rely on one being provided. Then there's the towel bale in case theirs is the scratchy kind and a pamper package to restore my inner calm and breathe new life into my soul. Obviously, I need the scented candles to create the aura and wellies. Did I mention them? They take up rather a lot of space you know, along with the assorted trainers for different purposes and strappy heels in case I go somewhere posh. I mean, quite honestly, Freddie, I'm seriously wondering if I packed enough."

He groans and lies back on the bed and says irritably, "Well, I just brought the one bag. You can spend the next seven hours unpacking while I watch Netflix and chill."

He flicks on the television and leans back on the bed and I struggle to look away. Seeing him in bed like this, even though he is fully dressed, is making my heart flutter a little. Picturing me beside him in less clothing is making me sweat a little and I swallow hard as I manage to squeak, "Um, we will need to rethink the sleeping arrangements too. I mean, Sandra did say there was a cot available."

"A cot!" He blinks and says incredulously, "How old are you? You'll never fit into a cot."

"A cot bed, a fold up, blow up, oh I don't know what, but you'll have to take that."

"Why me, I'm bigger than you?"

"Because you are the man."

"What does that even mean? I'm the man so I should suck it up and rough it on the floor, while the smaller, more petite adult in the room gets the larger sleeping position. No, honey, we're sharing, end of. You can build a barricade down the middle, do whatever you want, but this bed is mine, I was here first."

Turning away, I try not to admit I'm more than happy about that. Sharing with Freddie is no real hardship. He's eye candy of the most delightful kind and if anything, it will help put me off him because I'm guessing if he snores or makes any other body noise, I will be put off him by nature, anyway.

Deciding to ignore him, I set about unpacking and am grateful for the wardrobe space. It doesn't take me long to fill it, and then I venture into the bathroom and look around with delight. Sandra was right, this is paradise because there is one of those footed baths that stands proudly in the middle of the room. She has left some gorgeous toiletries on the side and I am itching to relax in the deep bath, filled with scented water. After the day I've had, I can't wait.

Quickly, I grab my fluffy bathrobe and towelling slippers that I pinched from Luton Hoo spa day and grab my wash bag. Freddie doesn't even look up as I retrieve my book and pour myself a glass of complimentary wine that has been left on the side. I hand him one and say quickly, "Here you go, I'm just going for a pamper. I will probably be two hours, so don't worry and think I've drowned, I'm reading."

"Two hours!" He stares at me in shock and I giggle. "Yes, two hours, nothing wrong with a bit of 'me' time, you should try it one day."

A flicker of interest sparks in his eyes and I say quickly, "When I'm not around though. Anyway, I should be, um, going."

I make a quick exit and leave him reclining on the bed and try to shake the man from my mind. I need this time alone to set my defences in place. I wanted this break to re-evaluate my life and change direction. With him here it's reaffirming what an idiot I am because if I don't stop myself, I will make all the same mistakes again with him.

Hot steamy deep bath √
Bubbles √
Wine√
Book√
Scented candles √
Silence√

As I lower myself into a little corner of paradise, I finally relax. The journey, the encounter with the farmers, the weird sleeping arrangements, the psychotic Kevin, all cease to matter as I relax with a glass of average wine and a good book and lose myself in another world.

~

"Susie, hurry up I need the loo."

"What?" I can't believe it; I've only been in here for half an hour and he's already battering the door down.

"Sorry, honey, but I can't hold on."

Muttering under my breath, I put the book down and struggle out of the bath, quickly grabbing my towel and cursing him in twenty different languages in my head, despite the fact that I only know one properly.

Stomping over to the door, dripping water as I go, I open it and say tightly, "Hurry up then."

He stares around in amazement. "Wow, you know how to relax, I'm impressed."

I feel quite proud of myself as I see the room through his eyes. The steam is hot and welcoming and scented with lime and basil. The candles that flicker on every surface dress the room with spa like decadence, and the wine on the side is the ultimate in indulgence.

He shakes his head and says hopefully, "Room for one more?"

I'm not sure why, but I hesitate and grasp my towel a little tighter as images of him shirtless spring to mind and I hate the fact my perfect bathroom relaxation moment would be more than enhanced with him in it. From the look on his face he is a mind reader as well because the sexy smirk he has obviously perfected is making me grow a little heated, so I revert to the only defence I have and say irritably, "Definitely not. You have two minutes, tops."

Turning my back, I leave him to it and retreat to the

safety of the bedroom, wondering how on earth this is going to work.

I know what I'm like and he is an object of mass destruction where my heart is concerned. Why couldn't it have been one of the fossil hunters? Why him, a man with a sexy smile and a body that was made to ruin women everywhere? The fact he's good company doesn't help because he's obviously funny, intelligent and a man I would love to spend time with ordinarily, but that's not why I'm here. I'm here to get away from my poor judgement where the opposite sex is concerned. Rediscover the woman I should be and steer away from the road to ruin that I appear to have stumbled upon.

"All done."

I look up and realise I've migrated to the bed and sit clutching my towel around me, leaving a worrying damp patch on the edge.

The steam from the room has caused my face to flush and now I'm out of it I shiver a little as the draft hits me. Freddie smiles and says apologetically, "You're cold, I'm sorry, I ruined your moment. Would you like me to top the bath up with hot water, it's the least I can do?"

"No, um, thanks, I've got it."

Quickly, I scramble to my feet, desperately holding onto the towel and avoiding eye contact, head back to the sanctuary of the bathroom a confused woman. I knew this was a huge mistake because I am not to be trusted. My heart is just too desperate to find someone to love, and men like Freddie Carlton are the love you and leave them kind. I must be strong and distance myself from him at all costs, which is a bit difficult when we are set to be joined at the hip this week.

Honestly, I could really get Kevin to murder Polly!

CHAPTER 8

Somehow my latest romance book isn't cutting it. I couldn't get past the image of Freddie playing the hero in the book and with a sigh of frustration, I curse my bad luck and my soon to be ex-best friend. Cutting my losses, I dress ready for bed and hope that Freddie is asleep because this proves to be the most awkward night ever.

Making sure to choose the maximum layers possible to sleep in tonight, I brush my teeth and venture into the room nervously to find Freddie lying in bed already with his hands behind his head, propped up watching a film. The trouble is, he obviously doesn't believe in pyjama tops and is bare chested, and my mind is suddenly filled with a buzzing sound that is making me confused because I just can't stop staring.

He smirks making me even more annoyed and I snap, "Haven't you got something you could wear in bed, I mean, it's a little disrespectful don't you think?"

"Not really, I always sleep like this, although I did keep on my boxers as a concession and anyway, you appear to be wearing enough clothes for both of us, don't you get hot?"

"No." I'm such a liar because the sight of him is making me feel very hot indeed, and it's not because of the clothes.

"Anyway, what's wrong with what I'm wearing, it's called lounge wear, it's all the rage, in case you were asking?"

"Not really, it looks uncomfortable to me, I like freedom when I sleep."

"For what?"

He winks and I grumble, "Never mind, anyway, what's your plan?"

He raises his eyes and I say crossly, "For keeping your distance, didn't you say something about a barricade?"

"No, I said you could build one if you wanted to, I'm fine as we are."

Frantically, I look around for some kind of impenetrable defence to separate the bed, but there are only hundreds of scatter cushions that will have to do. Grabbing an armful, I start launching them at him like torpedoes and say in what I hope is a no-nonsense brisk kind of voice, "Here you go, start erecting your walls."

He smirks and I groan. "Come on, hurry up."

He starts to laugh and I direct one of the cushions at his head, which wipes the smile off his face momentarily.

Somehow, he returns the cushion which hits me square in the face and I take it as a declaration of war and start gathering my troops and launching each scatter cushion at him with a rapid-fire movement.

Despite myself, I start to giggle because this is just too funny and as it erupts into a full-blown war, I'm pretty sure the noise we are making would wake the next county.

Before long, he advances and all of my cushions return in one heap of trouble and suddenly, I find my defences infiltrated as he tickles me relentlessly until I gasp, "Ok, you win, enough."

"Really, I win."

"Yes, please stop."

I can't stop giggling and the tears are rolling down my face as he laughs and carries on. Pushing him away, I shake my head and gasp, "Ok, fun's over, let's start building our defences."

To his credit, he does as I ask and we soon have quite an impressive line of defence down the middle of the bed.

As I hop into my side, I could almost be alone and feel a lot happier now I don't have to worry about touching any part of him inadvertently in the night.

"Happy, babe?"

"Yes, thanks."

He jumps in beside me and the bed sags a little and as he turns out the light, it casts an eerie shadow in the room. It illuminates the darkness and I'm guessing the moon must be pretty impressive out there, so I jump out of bed quickly to see if I'm right.

"What's up?"

Freddie sounds worried and I say quickly, "I'm checking on the moon, I think it may be one of those harvest ones, you know, the impressive one that makes your wishes come true."

"Do you really believe that?"

"Yes, of course, why, don't you?"

"Never gave it much thought."

As I reach the window, I pull back the curtain and peer out and as I thought, the moon is magnificent, making me gasp.

"Freddie, come and look, it's one of those blood-red ones, this is special."

He appears beside me and says, "Wow, impressive. What does this one mean?"

"I'm not sure, but it's kind of amazing. Maybe we should make that wish in case it does have magical powers."

"Ok, you go first."

Squeezing my eyes tightly shut, I think about my greatest wish that has never changed in all the years I've been wishing. Unless you count when I was a child and it usually involved the latest toy. Now it's much the same, although this time the toy is real and of the male variety. In my mind, I plead with the love gods and offer a silent prayer. 'Please deliver my happy ever after. Please make him caring, loving and loyal. Don't deliver me one that will let me down and run off at the first opportunity and please make it soon because I'm getting on a bit and want to get started on my family. Oh, and while you're at it, please can I have health for me and my family and world peace. Thank you love god, Susie Mahoney.'

Opening my eyes, I say breathlessly, "Your turn."

"What, have you been already?"

"Yes."

"What did you wish for?"

"I can't tell you because then it wouldn't come true."

"Ok, but I'm guessing you prayed for a man."

"What makes you think that?"

"Because that's all women want, isn't it? It's all any of us really want, come to think of it."

"A man, you surprise me, Freddie."

He nudges me and I laugh softly. For the first time since I met him, he sounds a little wistful as he says, "Isn't that the dream - to find true love? Someone to wake up with and make your day count for something amazing. A shared dream and a love so deep it stands whatever life throws at it. Someone to be your best friend, your lover, the mother of your children and your emotional rock."

I feel breathless as he opens up a little part of his soul to me and I step inside, blinded by his words. I whisper, "Yes, we all want that, Freddie."

For a moment, we stand shoulder to shoulder gazing at

the blood-red moon and there is silence all around. Not an uncomfortable one, one that is probably the most comfortable you will ever find. Despite everything, I do like Freddie Carlton, he makes it impossible not to, which is why this week is going to be so hard. I am the problem between us because I'm determined not to let him in. I need someone else, someone I can rely on and someone for keeps, not just a wild fling in the country and I must be firm about that.

I shiver a little and he says softly, "Come on, let's turn in for the night. You must be exhausted."

Nodding, I take one last look at the moon and scramble under the duvet and sigh with contentment as the soft pillow cradles my head in luxury.

The bed dips beside me and Freddie murmurs, "Good night, Susie."

"Good night, Freddie."

As I lie on my back, I say in a whisper, "You didn't make your wish."

From out of the darkness comes a soft voice, "Don't worry, Susie, I wished really hard and if you're right, I may get my happy ever after, after all."

CHAPTER 9

I wake from a deep sleep filled with happy dreams. I can't remember what they were, but they have left a warm feeling inside me and for a moment I think I'm back home in bed. Then a grunt beside me makes me stiffen as I remember I slept with a stranger last night, who by the sounds of it, is also just about to wake up.

"Morning, Susie, did you sleep well?"

His voice is husky and laced with sleepy contentment, and I feel my heart beating inside me with the promise of giving out on me before the week is up. Steeling myself for another day of resistance, I say calmly, "Yes, did you?"

"Like a log, although I must say, I could eat a rabid rat right now."

"Do you think we've missed breakfast? I mean, it's rather bright in here and we may have overslept."

"No, it's just 8 o'clock. Do you want to use the bathroom first, or shall I?"

"I'll go."

Quickly, I scramble out of bed and make a run for it, hoping he gets dressed while I'm away, and as I slam the bathroom door behind me, I take a moment to gather my traitorous thoughts. Looking in the mirror, I see a pale reflection staring back at me and I shake my head and point at it angrily. 'Oh no you don't my girl. Stay focused with your eye on the prize, and that doesn't mean that man next door. No, steel your heart and guard your soul because this week is a test of endurance, a man detox, a journey of self-discovery and building of walls. Redefine your goals and discover your inner peace because you need a break from matters of the heart for the sole reason you can't be trusted.'

Feeling a little better about my 'self' pep talk, I clean my teeth, brush my hair and use the toilet, before heading back into the room to decide on an outfit for the day. I'm surprised to see Freddie pressed up against the headboard with the covers raised to his chin, looking utterly traumatised.

"What's the matter?"

His eyes are wide and fearful, and I feel a prickle of unease as he nods towards the door.

"Can you get rid of it?"

"Rid of what?" I flick my attention to the door but can't see anything there.

"What are you looking at, Freddie, because unless you're seeing ghosts or something, there's nothing there?"

"Look above, in the corner, it's there."

Raising my eyes, I look up and let out a piercing scream.

"Oh my god, no, Freddie, do something."

He shakes his head vigorously as I jump into the bed beside him and pull the duvet up to my chin and say with my voice shaking, "What are we going to do?"

We both stare in horror at the hideous creature weaving its web above the only way out of here and Freddie whispers, "We need to remove it, I can't stay here with that – creature in the same room."

"Well, I can't deal with it, you'll have to."

"Me, why me?"

"Because you're the man, it's what they do."

"That again. I may be the man, but women want equality these days, so it's up to you to deal with it because you would be letting the side down if you didn't."

"Who said I was a feminist; you deal with it?"

Freddie yells and I grab hold of his arm, "What?"

"It moved." He hisses and we both stare at the spider in horror as it moves slowly down the door.

"Freddie, please do something, it's coming for us. It senses we are weak and is under attack."

"I'm sorry, Susie, but I have serious arachnophobia. I'm afraid you will have to step up and do the dirty deed."

"Me! Are you insane? I don't step up, I back away. Anyway, you live alone. What do you normally do when a spider comes to visit?"

He stares at me in disbelief. "I live in Surrey, Susie. We have people that come and take the creature away. No, this time I insist you deal with it."

"I can't." My voice shakes and I stare at him in horror. "What are we going to do?"

He looks around, still holding the duvet to his neck and whispers, "Do you think you could crawl through the window and run for help?"

I stare across at the window and shake my head. "I don't think so. By the looks of them they aren't wide enough. Maybe it's a security device to keep intruders out."

My stomach growls and I groan in despair. "Do you think we'll die in here?"

"I think we must prepare ourselves for that."

We share a desperate look and then scream loudly as the door flies open and the strangest sight frames the doorway.

An elderly woman dressed in lycra is standing there

looking at us with interest. Her hair is piled in a messy bun on top of her head and her lips are painted bright red. She has some huge designer sunglasses perched on her head and if this woman exercises, it's not a good advert because the rolls of fat create an interesting display under her cropped top that is doing little to contain the force of gravity that is pulling down her huge breasts. However, that's not the worst of it because I hear Freddie gasp in horror beside me as we watch the spider take up residence on her messy bun and we both just stare at her in abject horror.

"Is everything ok, I heard screaming?"

I open my mouth but no words come as I see the spider crawling around the haphazard hair and Freddie says weakly, "Sp, sp, sp…"

"I'm Lizzie, by the way, Sandra's mother. I must say I've been dying to grab a look at you, young man. Sandra told me we had a hot guy come to stay, and I wondered if you fancied getting a sweat on with me."

She winks and if it wasn't for the spider, I would be in hysterics at the expression on Freddie's face.

"But…"

"Shall we say ten minutes? I'll start running and wait for you to catch me handsome. Then I'm all yours."

She winks and as she turns to go, I muster some courage from out of nowhere and shout, "There's a spider."

"Where?" She turns and looks around her as Freddie nudges me. Throwing him a furious look, I feel quite proud of myself for alerting the frail woman to the possible danger ahead of her. I mean, anything could happen and as she jogs on the spider could run down her face and cause a heart attack. No, this is my civic duty and so I say faintly, "Um, on your head."

Freddie grips my arm hard as she reaches up and ferrets around in her hair, and we watch in horror as she closes her hand around the spider and lifts it clean off before studying it with interest.

"Ooh, a big one, I do so love a nice big one."

She winks at Freddie who looks as if he may faint and not because of the spider and she moves a little nearer, spider in hand.

"Surely a big…" Her eyes lower to the trembling jelly beside me and winks. "A big strapping lad like you isn't afraid of a little biddy spider?"

She advances and we both cower in our bed in utter terror, both conscious there is no way of escape.

She laughs loudly and shakes her head. "Goodness, if I wasn't so curious you would have been there all day and missed Sandra's award winning breakfast. I say award winning, she won first place in the local battle of the bed and breakfasts, you'd think she won an Oscar the way she goes on about it."

She stares at the creature wriggling in her hand and smiles. "Maybe I'll keep you and call you Oscar. I'm sure you'll be much better company than the major. Have you seen a man marching around here this morning, he went out for his constitutional an hour ago and hasn't come back? Mind you, it wouldn't be the first time he's strayed. Me either come to think of it."

She winks at Freddie again, but we are failing to see anything but the grotesque creature struggling to free itself from her grasp.

As she turns to leave, she says casually, "You know, I heard a fun fact about spiders. Spiders will lay between 2 and 1000 eggs, depending on the species. I wonder if she's managed that since she's been here."

She grins and heads out the way she came, thankfully taking the spider with her, and Freddie stares at me in horror.

"1000, surely not."

"Even 2 is too many. What are we going to do?"

The door slams and we hear Lizzie laughing as she supposedly jogs off and Freddie groans. "I'm not sure if I can stay here now, I feel violated."

"What, the spider or the crazy woman?"

I start to giggle more with relief now the trauma has passed and Freddie shakes his head. "Come on, let's get out of here and grab some of that award winning breakfast. I hope she serves alcohol with it."

He heads off to the bathroom and I stare at the web in horror and think of another 1000 reasons why this was a bad idea.

CHAPTER 10

It feels extremely awkward when we venture into the dining room because just about every pair of eyes swivel in our direction. Not only are Freddie and I feeling very fragile right now, but we are apparently the last ones up because most of the others are finishing off.

Sandra walks in with a teapot in her hand and smiles her welcome.

"There you are, I trust you slept well."

"Lovely, thank you."

Freddie and I say it at the same time, and I groan inside. How is this happening? It appears that Freddie is shaping up to be a carbon copy of me. Me in a man's body, how is this possible?

We weave our way sheepishly through the tables, and I almost wilt under the glare the woman gives me as she notices her husband's interested look. The fossil men are nudging each other and failing to disguise the humour in their smiles and I want them all to leave – immediately.

Remembering the racket we made last night during the

pillow fight and the loud screams this morning, I'm guessing they have all come to completely the wrong conclusions.

As we settle in our seats, Sandra beams. "I heard you met my mother, she's a character for sure, just try to ignore her, we do."

"Oh, um, well, she seemed really lovely, Sandra."

Freddie nods. "Wonderful, you are, um, very lucky."

She rolls her eyes and sets the teapot down on the table.

"Listen, she's harmless enough, just of the generation who have no filter. She may be a little inappropriate at times, but means well. Don't mind her and just get on with your day. Oh, and if you see an elderly gentleman in full military attire, that's her husband. Same goes for him, just smile and walk on past. Now, let me take your breakfast order, you must be starving."

The room is once again silent, and I shift awkwardly on my seat as I order the full English with granary toast and a side of pancakes.

Freddie nods his approval. "Same."

As she leaves us to it, I lean in and whisper, "Do you get the feeling the others don't approve of us?"

He nods and leans even closer and hisses, "Those guys are practically drooling over you, you should thank your lucky stars you have someone to protect you."

He raises his eyes and I look past him at the table of fossil men who are now openly staring with what appears to be fascination on their faces. My heart sinks when I realise they think I'm sort of paid sex worker after our stunt last night, and if I was, I could definitely clean up here.

Leaning back, I feel a little powerful if I'm honest and quite happy to take on the burden. It makes me feel wicked, devilish and a little extreme and I'm quite liking this new power I have over men.

Tossing my hair back, I smile in their direction and see six faces blush all at once.

Fighting back the giggles, I look at Freddie and smile triumphantly and he just rolls his eyes and reaching out, takes my hand and kisses it like a gentleman.

I'm so shocked, I just stare at him and hiss, "What are you doing?"

"Warning them off and marking my territory."

"That's a little primitive, isn't it?"

"What can I say, I'm a caveman."

His eyes twinkle and I have to admit I'm actually winning at life right now and even risk a smile to the woman at the next table and say loudly, "Good morning, lovely day."

She nods and smiles tightly and her husband, at least I think he is, says pleasantly, "Yes, we're heading to Durdle Door, have you been there yet?"

He winces and I expect it's because she's just kicked him sharply under the table and I smile. "Sounds good, maybe we'll go too."

I stare at Freddie and smile. "What do you say, fancy a hike?"

His face falls and I wonder if I've got this all wrong. Maybe he's planning on heading home after all, and suddenly I feel a little foolish.

He shrugs and shakes his head. "Sorry, honey, I've got an appointment I can't get out of. You go though, have fun."

Forgetting the couple at the next table, I lean in and whisper, "Have you really, or are you leaving?"

"No, of course not, I really do."

"Since when?"

"Since yesterday. I arranged a meeting at the pub we went to. It will probably take a few hours so you should go and explore, maybe recharge your inner zen like you intended to."

I smile, but inside I'm on code red. He has a meeting, an appointment, a date perhaps? It's that sassy barmaid, I just know it. They probably arranged a rendezvous when I went to the ladies. I'm such a fool, of course they did, it's why she looked at me as if I'm public enemy number one.

Suddenly, a voice reaches us from the fossil table as one of them says loudly, "You can come with us if you like."

Looking up in surprise, I see them all looking at me hopefully and Freddie snorts before quickly disguising it into a cough. Feeling annoyed at him for arranging a date behind my back, I toss my hair back and throw them my most seductive smile, noting how they turn as red as a tomato in one collective burst of colour.

"Lovely, thank you. I have a car if I can help with a lift."

"No need, we have a minibus. Matty can drive, you can sit in the back next to me."

The man who spoke looks at the others triumphantly and my heart sinks. Great, this is all I need, an excursion with the cast of the Big Bang Theory.

Freddie laughs and can't disguise the amusement in his voice as he says loudly, "Sounds good, you should go honey, have fun and who knows, you may discover a new dinosaur."

Sandra chooses the moment to return with our breakfasts and says with interest, "You should venture to Seaton, there's a new museum there with so many interesting fossils and information on the history of the area. Such fun."

Shrinking down my seat, I throw Freddie a furious look. Thanks a lot, just brilliant.

If Sandra's breakfast is award winning, it's lost on me because I can't register anything other than the despair I'm feeling at the thought of the day ahead. Freddie is off to an illicit meeting and I'm heading off with six strangers in a minibus to look for God only knows what.

This trip is not shaping up well at all.

CHAPTER 11

I'm not sure why the fossil hunters are looking at me with a mixture of horror and fascination when I meet them in the courtyard. Freddie has left already, which gave me time to get suitably attired for the day ahead.

I see them assessing me and this time not in a good way and wonder if the velvet leggings and short faux fur jacket are a step too far with my snow boots. The guy who invited me says slightly nervously, "Do you have any walking boots, maybe an anorak and a rucksack filled with an ordinance survey map and a packed lunch? I have a spare bottle of water if you need it, but that's all I'm afraid."

The others look uncomfortable as I grip my favourite handbag a little tighter and say slightly hysterically, "An anorak?"

I actually feel faint at the thought, and their designated spokesperson nods reassuringly. "I have one if you need one, it's my spare."

"NO!"

He looks a little taken aback and I lower my voice. "No,

thank you. I'm good thanks. I mean, I usually go for walks dressed like this and it is a walk, isn't it?"

I feel slightly nervous because what if we're doing some kind of extreme activity that I'm not prepared for?

"Well, technically yes, but you could get a little dirty if you decide to investigate an area."

"Why, what will that involve?"

I'm a little confused because in my mind the only area I'll be investigating is the local pub for lunch after a brisk walk on the beach. I mean, how messy can that be?

One of the others shouts, "It's ok Thomas, we have some spare overalls in the back and a pair of wellingtons. We really should get going before we lose the best spot."

Thomas nods and smiles apologetically, and I hold out my hand. "I'm sorry, I'm Susie, and I'm guessing you're Thomas. Maybe we should go around the circle of trust and introduce ourselves."

The others look as if they don't have time for such simple pleasantries, but Thomas nods and points everyone out. "Ok, I'm Thomas and the driver is Matty." He points to the rest, who look a little uncomfortable as they shuffle on their feet beside the minibus. "Oliver, Jacob, George and Noah. We are the Windsor contingent and are regulars to the Lyme Bay fossil convention. It's the highlight of our year."

"Super."

I smile, but any self-satisfaction I had is dwindling fast as I anticipate a day of boredom followed by super boredom.

Miserably, I clamber in after Thomas and belt up, deciding to make the most of what I must remind myself was a kind invitation.

"So, where are we going, the museum?"

I'm almost hopeful because I'm guessing any museum would have a welcoming coffee shop with a gift shop attached, but Thomas shakes his head and says with some excitement. "It's not far, a place called Abbotsbury. Chesil beach, to be precise. It's a great area for metal detecting and we had hoped to get a few hours in before the convention catch up at the pub in West Bay."

"Super."

My heart sinks even further and I just pray they drop me off before the convention catch up because even with the promise of a pub, it appears to be a step too far.

Luckily, it isn't far to Chesil beach and I look with delight at the one of the prettiest villages I have ever seen.

Art galleries, a pottery, a sweet little village store and a pub. Bingo. "This looks nice."

I feel quite pleased with myself as Thomas nods. "It's a great place. The beach isn't far."

We tear off down a dusty track and I see the sea sparkling like a fine jewel in the distance. Above it is a tall hill with what appears to be an ancient monument on top of it staring majestically out to sea and I say with interest, "What's that?"

Jacob consults his iPad and reads, "St Catherine's Chapel. According to the English Heritage site, St Catherine's Chapel was built by the monks of nearby Abbotsbury Abbey as a pilgrimage chapel. Virtually unaltered since, it is one of a handful of chapels of this kind which are located outside the precincts of the monasteries that built them. Its isolated setting allowed the monks to withdraw from the monastery during Lent for private prayer and meditation. The dedication of the chapel to St Catherine of Alexandria is rare, but her cult was one of the most popular in medieval England. As the chapel overlooks the sea, it is likely to have been used as a beacon or sea-mark after the Dissolution, which may have ensured its preservation. In later times a navigation light was kept burning at the top of its stair turret."

He breaks off and shifts his glasses before looking at me and smiling. "This may interest you, Susie, there's a legend of

St Catherine and it concerns the fireworks known as Catherine wheels used to commemorate her torture in the 3rd century AD, when the Roman Emperor Maximus I ordered her to be broken on a wheel set with sword points for protesting about the persecution of Christians. An angel is said to have broken the wheel, and after her subsequent execution Catherine's body was said to have been conveyed to the heights of Mount Sinai by angels. She became the patron saint of virgins, particularly those in search of husbands, and it was the custom until the late 19th century for the young women of Abbotsbury to go to the chapel and invoke her aid. They would put a knee in one of the wishing holes in the south doorway, their hands in the other two holes, and make a wish."

"Why would that concern me?"

Thomas laughs. "No reason, it's just that you're the only one of us who's a girl, so it applies to you more than us."

"Oh, I see."

I feel a little foolish and smile brightly. "Sounds amazing, maybe I should check it out while I'm here."

"I think you could walk up to it if you get bored with metal detecting. We could meet you there when we've finished."

"Or the local pub, that looked nice."

Thomas nods, and I feel extremely pleased with myself for covering all my options. Yes, St Catherine's Chapel is a godsend; a beacon of hope to all single, um, virgins everywhere and I would be a fool not to pay my respects before venturing down the hill and partaking of a hearty cream tea, or a dram of whisky at the cosy pub I saw, while I wait for them to pick me up.

CHAPTER 12

Chesil beach is breath-taking. The sun is shining and catches the waves making the sea sparkle and the crash of the waves to the shore, coupled with the call of the seagulls, reminds me how far I've come from my hometown of Slipend. In fact, it now seems a world away and I've decided that my spiritual home is Dorset. I feel so happy here and it's as if I have no worries and life is easy.

George walks with me while the others fiddle around with their metal detectors, and I laugh to myself because he obviously feels extremely uncomfortable.

"So, tell me, George, what do you do for a living, other than treasure hunting, of course?"

I smile to make him more comfortable and he blinks and says softly, "I'm a computer engineer."

"That sounds amazing."

"It's ok. It pays the bills."

"Have you always wanted to do that?"

He shakes his head and looks a little wistful. "I've always wanted to be an archaeologist."

"Then why didn't you?"

"Because it was difficult and computers were always my thing."

"Could you still do it, become an archaeologist, I mean?"

"Possibly, mind you, I'm not sure I can be bothered to change direction now."

"Why not?"

I stare at him in surprise as he shrugs. "It's just easier to keep it as a hobby and enjoy it as an obsession." He looks a little awkward and says in a rather high-pitched voice, "So, what about you, what do you do for a living?"

"Oh, this and that." I'm a little vague because I'm doubting that George, or any of them, would understand my own choice of profession and I laugh with a little embarrassment.

"Goodness, it looks as if they've found something already."

We see the rest of the group huddled around something and George says quickly, "Shall we see what they've found?"

Feeling way more interested than I thought I would, we head over and see Noah holding up a metal object, while the rest of the guys look on with interest.

"What is it?"

I almost can't wait to find out. Maybe they've discovered an ancient coin or a medieval piece of armour from the suit of the fallen. Perhaps it's an ancient artefact preserved for our pleasure, but Jacob says with a little disappointment, "I think it's part of a boat. I'm not sure what part, but we should take it away for analysis just in case.

"Oh." I stare at the rusty bit of metal with disappointment, my earlier thrill diminishing under the ordinary.

Noah shakes his head. "Come on, keep going. I researched the area and there were several shipwrecks in this location and I'm pretty sure there must be some form of treasure still around. It's also been around since the ice age, so who knows what wonders lie beneath the shingle? Keep going guys, there must be something."

They nod and split up and I soon hear various sounds coming from their equipment and despite myself, I find I'm quite enjoying the experience. Maybe it's the unknown, the hint of expectation that something life changing may be just a few pebbles underground.

Thomas falls into step beside me and says kindly, "Would you like a go, Susie?"

"Great, can I?"

He hands me the equipment and I take great pleasure in walking beside him while he explains the intricacies of metal detecting. In fact, I may even get one myself because it's giving me a thrill I never thought I'd experience and has opened my eyes a little.

However, after finding a £1-coin, two beer caps and a metal belt buckle, I'm feeling a little despondent and soon lose interest.

Deciding to call it quits, I say apologetically, "Listen, do you mind if I head back to that sweet little village we passed. I'll meet you in the pub if you like, don't hurry, take your time."

Oliver looks worried. "Would you like me to walk with you?"

"No thanks, I'll be fine, I'm just interested to explore the area a little."

He nods. "Ok, but give me your number and call if you need a lift."

We swap numbers and I leave them to it, and despite the fact they've been good company, I relish the solitude because this is what I've been craving since I arrived. I thought this trip would be a time for reflection and self-analysis. A time to set new goals in place and make a new life plan. Things haven't really gone according to plan, and I'm grateful for a bit of alone time to gather my thoughts and take some much-needed time out.

Thirty minutes later and I'm feeling a little uncomfortable and wishing I hadn't worn ski boots and a faux fur jacket. It's actually really warm, and the jacket is a little cumbersome to carry. The ski boots aren't much protection against the stones on the beach, and my feet are throbbing by the time I make it to the track leading to the village. I'm obviously out of shape because I've got a stitch, and it's painful to walk, and I'm sure I'm developing a blister on my feet that is making me hobble a little.

I don't pass many other people, which is quite a good thing really because I'm now in no mood for small talk. I almost consider calling Oliver and beg to be rescued, but something, pride perhaps, is making me forge on ahead, determined to do something different for a change.

I decide to head up the hill to the chapel and see what it's all about, and as I pass several sheep, I feel sorry for them in their huge woolly coats. I know how hot they must be and smile sympathetically as I pass. Now I have a destination goal I am keen to get there because my feet are throbbing, I'm melting under my layers and my muscles have awakened and are protesting at this barbaric treatment where they are usually left to their own devices and are not required to work much.

However, as soon as I reach the top, all is forgotten as I stare at a view that will live in my memory forever. It's as if I'm on top of the world as I look around me, the sea on one side and a beautiful little valley behind, where thatched cottages nestle, their chimneys making me long for the smell of wood smoke and a buttery crumpet to take the edge off my appetite.

St Catherine's Chapel stands beside me, wrapped in history and promising a link to the past as I follow in the footsteps of the virgins that came before me, to see what treasures lie within its walls and it is with an air of expectation that I head inside.

CHAPTER 13

There's not a lot here, actually. I'm disappointed as I make my way inside what is actually a very small space. There's an eerie silence inside, with only the occasional gust of wind that passes through the cracks in the walls and small leaded windows. A large magnificent window at one end stands proudly overlooking the lush countryside, letting some form of light into a place that was abandoned centuries ago. The floor is uneven and covered in ancient stone, and it's just a shell of what it once was all those years ago.

It's strange being the only one here and I imagine the ghosts of previous visitors through the ages all around me as I step back in time.

Despite the fact there's not a lot here, I love it and take a moment to appreciate the simplicity of a life that needs no modern convenience. Nature and man living side by side through the ages and I wonder what secrets this chapel protects as it stands majestically on its hill, surrounded by sheep.

For a moment, I lean against one of the ancient walls and

relish a moment of relaxation. I'm actually worn out and grateful for a moment to gather my thoughts along with my breath and think about why I'm here. Life hasn't been kind to me lately on the romantic front. This seems as good a place as any to think about that, because this is where women have come through time to pray for something better.

Thinking about Kevin and the drama that went with that particular relationship, leaves a bitter taste in my mouth. I really thought I loved him. He was everything I always wished for and I couldn't get enough of him. When he turned out to be married with his first child on the way, I thought my heart was broken forever. Then when he offered to put me up in a flat and use me for sex, the penny dropped, leaving me feeling worthless and cheap.

The trouble is, I've been feeling that a lot lately. I think I met Scott on the rebound and he appeared to offer me everything I was looking for. We met when I escorted him to a party in London one night. Strictly business that ended up with me breaking my golden rule, not to mix business with pleasure. There's a reason why I'm ashamed to admit what I do for a living because people would be right to judge me based on that experience alone. To some, being an escort is one step away from prostitution, as Kevin demonstrated when he played with my feelings so cruelly. When Scott happened, I fell into the trap I always steered away from and actually slept with a client, making me into something I never wanted to be.

Being an escort was never on the careers list at school but was easy money and got me out most evenings. All I am required to do is make polite conversation and act as arm candy for men who need a companion, a plus one to take to dinner, film premiers, and business functions. I actually love my job, or should I say loved because after Scott and Kevin, it has lost a little of its shine.

Scott wanted the whole experience. To his credit, he loved me. I think he still does because he went a step further than most and proposed. For a while, I got caught up in the dream and thought it was what I wanted too. He was rich, successful and good looking. I would be assured of a good life with him with everything I could wish for, but one thing, I didn't love him. In fact, he bored me and was so serious. There were no laughs and no spontaneity, which is why I am trying so hard to resist my feelings for Freddie. He ticks absolutely every box but one. He's a player, it's obvious by the fact he can't stop flirting with just about every girl he lays eyes on. I hate thinking of him with the sassy barmaid, probably cosying up together right now in a little alcove in the local pub. It's not that he owes me anything, we are strangers after all, but a little part of me feels as if he betrayed me.

Sighing, I look around me and offer a silent payer to Saint Catherine.

'Please help me find love.'

All around the wind is my only companion as the chapel stands silent and proud, and I feel a little embarrassed asking Saint Catherine for anything. I'm not the vestal virgin who prays for a man. I'm the scarlet woman who doesn't deserve one. In fact, I deserve everything I get because I can't make a life choice to save my tainted soul.

Sighing, I look around and spy the little alcove that Jacob spoke about in the south doorway. As I walk over to it, I smile to myself. Maybe I should get the full Saint Catherine's experience and do what many have done before me. Pray hard for my dreams to come true and find my one true love, or at least someone I could grow old with and not resort to murdering him after two years.

Feeling a little foolish, I sink to my knees into one of the wishing holes and scramble around to find the ones for my hands.

Trying not to mind that it's seriously dusty and my velvet leggings are probably caked in mud right now, I close my eyes and summon the goddess of love to do my bidding and whisper, "Dear Saint Catherine, I fall upon your mercy and beg for help. Please help me find love. He doesn't even have to be rich, just kind, funny, good looking obviously and somebody who finishes my sentences and checks all my boxes. Someone I can grow old with and walk through life holding their hand, knowing they will always catch me when I fall. Someone who laughs at my stupid jokes and listens when I need to let it all out. A man who shares my dreams and doesn't judge me and someone who makes every second I live count for something amazing."

For some reason, the entire time I offered my wish, I could only see Freddie in my mind. I'm not even sure why because I came to my decision early on that he was definitely *not* the one. Life with him would be riddled with anxiety, wondering when he was going to move on with the next woman who caught his eye. No, I need someone more grown up, someone who knows what I want and will move heaven and earth to provide it for me.

Strangely, a lone tear splashes into the dirt at my feet and I'm surprised to see it. I don't cry; I'm not emotional, so why I feel it now is a mystery. Feeling a little ridiculous on my hands and knees, cowering in the dirt, I shift a bit and in doing so, cause some of the dust in the holes to crumble. I feel off balance and stumble a little, and my hands sink lower into the holes as I scrabble around in the dirt to save myself from collapsing on the ground in a dust heap.

As I do, something brushes against my hand and I die a little inside and offer a small scream into the silence.

As I pull back, something comes with me and as I blink in the dim light, it sparkles against my hand. I blink and then blink again and it's still there. A small metal object that dazzles me as the sun filters through the stone window and catches a corner of it.

My heart beats so fast I think it may give out on me as my fingers close around the small object and I lift it to the light.

A ring.

I peer closer and brush a little of the dirt off. Rocking to my knees, I sit and stare at something so magnificent my breath hitches and I gasp. Is that a diamond, it certainly looks like it? Holding it up to the light, I stare in amazement at a miracle. An actual diamond ring, lost and hidden in the walls of an ancient chapel.

I can't believe it.

My heart thumps as I stand and head outside into the light and dust it off a little. Now I'm in the open, I see I was right and a beautiful diamond ring sparkles in my hand. I can't resist the urge to try it on, and as it slips onto the third finger of my left hand, I hold it to the light and watch it flash in the sunlight. For some reason, the tears fall as I marvel at finding something so beautiful in a sacred place.

Then my common sense returns and the disappointment reminds me I must hand this in. Somebody has lost this, and it needs to be returned. However, this is my moment, my treasure, my find. I didn't need a metal detector to find something so special I will never forget this moment. I prayed for love and it sent me an engagement ring and that's a powerful message. Miracles do happen and it's happening right now.

Now all I need is the man to go with it.

CHAPTER 14

I feel like quite a celebrity as I sit nursing my aching feet in Sandra's cosy cottage with a steaming mug of tea on the table to my side. The fossil hunters, along with Sandra and Kevin are crowded around me, admiring the diamond ring I found.

"It's a miracle."

Sandra shakes her head and Kevin says slowly, "Do you think it would be morally wrong to keep it and say nothing?"

"Yes."

Sandra fixes him with a frown and Jacob nods. "I agree. It may belong to someone and looks as if it cost a lot of money."

Noah interrupts. "I say finders' keepers."

"Noah!" Oliver looks scandalised and I offer Noah a smile of support because the thought had crossed my mind on more than one occasion on the journey home.

The guys couldn't believe my find when they found me nursing a medicinal brandy in the local pub. In fact, I would go as far to say they looked green with envy because they ended up with the contents of a scrap merchants with nothing of value to show for their time and trouble.

Matty peers a little closer. "I think it's quite valuable. I mean, I don't know a lot about precious stones but this one has polished up well and if it's genuine, the size of the stone alone tells me it's worth several thousand pounds."

"And the rest." George is consulting his Apple watch and says, "If it's genuine, it could be worth close on a million."

We all stare at him in shock and he shrugs. "Ask google, it's all on there."

"I wonder who lost it?" Sandra looks thoughtful and I say sadly, "Whoever it was must really miss it. Maybe someone was doing the same as me and it fell off and she didn't realise it."

"Why would she?" Oliver looks surprised. "I mean, if she was already engaged, she wouldn't be praying for a man. It doesn't make sense."

"Good point." I stare at the ring in wonder and Kevin says firmly, "I think we should report it to the police. I'm guessing they have a set amount of time to find its owner and then it's yours if nobody comes forward. I think it's the right thing to do, unless…"

"What?" We all look at him with the expectation hanging heavily in the air and he whispers, "We say nothing. Let Susie keep it and sell it on the black market. It could be worth a pretty penny and it would help set her up for life."

"Honestly, Kevin, your morals need a little work. No, I think Susie's right, it could be some poor woman's treasure and we owe it to the spirit of St Catherine to find her. Call the police, Kevin, before we change our mind."

Kevin shrugs and heads outside to make the call and we stare at the ring in collective wonder.

"Is there an inscription, Susie?" Thomas says with

curiosity and I quickly slip it off my finger and see some tiny lettering on the inside of the ring. "There is."

I stare around the room, my eyes wide with excitement and they all shuffle a little closer. In fact, Matty is filming it to record the event for posterity in case the press get involved.

I read the tiny letters out in disbelief. "It belongs to somebody called Tiffany."

"Not somebody, dear." Sandra looks excited. "Tiffany is a make. Oh my god, a genuine Tiffany diamond ring, you are so lucky."

Matty taps on his Apple watch and says loudly, "Wow, Tiffany rings are expensive, I think you've got a good one as well. This could be worth a lot of money, Susie."

For a moment we stare at the ring, a little awestruck that such a small object holds such value.

Kevin returns and grumbles, "Bloody Lizzie has been in my man cave again."

Sandra rolls her eyes. "What now?"

"She's been rifling through my drawers, the woman's a liability."

"How do you know it was her?"

"She left her clothes on the chair."

We stare at him in shock as Sandra rolls her eyes. "Then count yourself lucky she's gone already. I don't suppose you saw anything of the major's in there, while you were at it."

"His shoes and braces."

Thomas catches my eye and the look on his face makes me giggle as Jacob says awkwardly. "I'm sorry, I wasn't going to say anything but I found them in my bed when I came back from tea last night."

The silence in the room is so tangible you need a knife to cut it as we struggle to deal with the trauma that must have involved.

Sandra sinks down heavily on the sofa and groans. "I thought they'd learned their lesson after the last time. I'll have a word but to be honest, I'm not sure how good it will be, so I suggest you all lock your doors to be on the safe side."

"I did."

Jacob looks traumatised as he whispers, "I did, I think they have a master key."

"Great, just great, I told you to keep it in the safe, Kevin. What am I going to do with the pair of them? They're only here because the McCarthy Stone thought they needed a little distance from the other residents after that Zoom quiz night went so badly wrong. Mrs Mortimer is still in hospital by all accounts."

"Why, what happened?"

I stare at Sandra in fascination as she lowers her voice. "My mother and the Major decided it would be fun to swap clothes, live on air. The trouble is, they removed every item they possessed and then proceeded to re-enact the Titanic by singing 'My Heart Will Go On.' The Major's hands weren't around her waist either. They nearly lost a few residents that night and have been banned from subsequent quiz nights. I don't know what I'm going to do with them. I really don't."

Despite how bad it is, I think we all want to laugh at the thought of it. Goodness, I hope I'm as active as Lizzie and the Major when I'm their age.

Kevin sighs and says almost apologetically.

"The police are sending someone here; they have a car in the area and it's a slow crime day, apparently, so they'll come and collect."

"Oh."

I feel a little sad now the deed is done. I know it was the right thing to do but it still hurts a little to think that my special find will be filed away in an evidence bag. Part of me hopes the owner doesn't claim it and yet the romantic in me hopes it does find its way home to the woman it was meant for.

CHAPTER 15

The police turn up an hour later and once again, we all crowd inside the cosy living room of the cottage. Seeing the police car gives me palpitations and I suppose it has a lot to do with PC Alex Murphy, who looks as if he's modelling the uniform. Even Sandra has gone all giggly and nothing is prising Lizzie away from his side for a second. I have to laugh as she gazes at him in adoration and keeps on placing her hand on his knee and squeezing it hard. He looks a little uncomfortable as her hand moves higher and after a potentially catastrophic final grope, Sandra shouts, "Lizzie, I can hear the Major calling."

PC Murphy looks eternally grateful as Lizzie looks annoyed. "I don't hear him."

"Because you're deaf. Now go and find him – immediately."

Lizzie leans closer to PC Murphy and whispers something that makes him look extremely uncomfortable and Sandra says tightly, "Now, mother."

Shrugging, Lizzie stands up and blows him a kiss as she

exits the room and he coughs awkwardly and then says quickly, "May I take the ring along with some details."

"Of course."

I feel a little sad to hand the ring over and Sandra shakes her head. "Do you think she'll get it back?"

"Possibly." He smiles at me and I see a devilish twinkle in his eye that I kind of like. In fact, the more I see of PC Murphy, the more I like him and the smile he is giving me tells me there's a little more than just a professional interest going on here.

For some reason, it makes me feel kind of strange inside. He's good looking, a respectable member of the community, and looks to be around my age. Maybe this ring always meant me to find a man like him. Perhaps PC Murphy is the pot of gold I was meant to find, but I feel a strange disappointment in that.

He pulls out a notebook and says in a deep, gorgeous voice. "If you could tell me the details of where and when you made the discovery. I also need your full name, address and telephone number."

He smiles warmly and I tell him what happened, while the others watch in fascination.

Once he has everything he needs, he stands and nods to the crowded room. "Well, I think that wraps this up. Thank you for handing this in, we will try to find the owner but if they can't be found, the ring will be returned to you."

"How long will that be?" Sandra asks the question I think we all want to know and he shrugs. "To be honest, we usually allow the finder to keep the item if they have done everything possible to find the owner. In this case, it's a valuable object found in a protected monument. It's a little more complicated, so I'm taking it to the station for advice. Hopefully, I should have an answer within a couple of days. I expect you will be returning home to…"

He consults his notebook. "Slipend."

I nod. "Yes, I'm only here for the week. Do you think I'll know by then?"

He smiles warmly, "I'll make it my personal business to keep you informed."

Sandra smiles and some of the guys look worried, but I like knowing I'll hear from him again. Obviously, I am out of control because I appear to be falling for just about any man who looks in my direction lately, which shows how desperate I am. Either that, or I'm still annoyed that Freddie has already started dating the locals without another thought for me, despite the fact I made it clear I wasn't interested.

Love is so complicated, it's no wonder I'm single.

He stands and snaps his notebook shut before placing it inside his coat and smiles.

"I think that will be all – for now. I won't take up any more of your time. Miss Mahoney..." He turns and smiles. "Please, may I have a word?"

I catch Sandra's eye and she smiles reassuringly and I feel my nerves fluttering around inside me like demented butterflies as I follow him outside. As we walk towards the police car, I am conscious of the man walking beside me. I'm not sure why I seem to be fixating on just about every man that crosses my path these days when I am supposed to be on a man detox. Maybe that's why, you always want what you shouldn't but Happy Ever After appears to be throwing temptation in my path at a rapid speed.

"You must be anxious."

"Excuse me."

I look at him in surprise as he interrupts my thoughts, and he smiles in a way that makes my heart race. "The ring, it's certainly a fine example of one."

"I guess, I never really thought about it."

"Don't worry, in my experience, these things are rarely

returned to their owner. Who knows how long it's been there, I mean, Saint Catherine's has been there for a considerable time already?"

"I doubt it. Tiffany rings surely haven't been around that long."

"You may be surprised at that." He smiles and a little piece of my heart melts as I look into his soulful brown eyes. PC Alex Murphy is good, I'll give him that. I expect he's used to women swooning at his feet around here and to be honest, I don't appear to be an exception to that, then again, my history on men is not a well calculated one, so I harden my heart and smile. "Yes, to be honest I'm a little uneducated when it comes to history. I've never really been interested in the past before, but since coming here it's opened my eyes a little. The area makes it impossible not to, and now I suppose I'll spend the next few days researching the life out of Saint Catherine's Chapel and Tiffany rings. Maybe it's a good thing for my education that I found it; it may broaden my mind a little."

We stop by his car and he leans back onto it and I swear my heart starts beating out of control because seeing a handsome man in uniform against an official car is a powerful aphrodisiac indeed.

"So…" He smiles and I can't think why I'm holding my breath, but I do as he stares at me with the same look I see on most of my client's faces when they leave me for the night. A mixture of friendship, disappointment and hope, all rolled into one powerful look and it throws me a little because I have no idea why PC Murphy is directing it at me.

We stand awkwardly for a few seconds in silence and then a car approaches taking our attention and I look up and see Freddie looking concerned as he stops beside us.

"Is everything ok, Suze?"

Seeing his concern makes my resolve melt a little more

and despite the fact I'm still annoyed he's been out with another woman, although I have absolutely no reason to be, I nod and smile feeling pleased to see him for some reason. "I'll explain later, it's fine."

He throws the police officer a worried look and PC Murphy pushes off the car and says quickly, "I should be going. It was nice to meet you, Miss Mahoney."

"Please, call me Susie."

"It was nice to meet you, Susie. I'll be in touch."

The smile he gives me makes my breath hitch a little because he is shaping up to be a man who could star in just about every fantasy I have, most of which involve his uniform and shaking myself, I nod and say slightly nervously, "Do you think I'll know anything before I leave?"

"When is that exactly?"

"Six days' time."

"Then I'll make it my priority to have an answer for you before then. Until the next time, Susie."

He winks and I watch him step into the police car with a mixture of relief and despair. Is it because he's taking my treasure with him, or is it because I feel as if destiny has delivered me my Happy Ever After as a double package in one day? I feel so confused and as he pulls away, I stand watching the car disappear, feeling a mix of emotions left in its exhaust fumes.

CHAPTER 16

*A*s soon as I turn to head back inside, Freddie appears as if by magic, looking concerned.

"I turn my back for five minutes and you're in trouble."

He smiles, but I see the anxiety on his face and I shake my head. "It's fine. Um, Freddie."

"Yes, babe."

"Do you fancy a walk?"

"Where to?"

"Maybe we should check out the beach, I haven't even made it that far yet, and it looks amazing."

"Sounds good."

He falls into step beside me and I'm not sure why I asked him but it feels as if I need someone to talk to and he is the closest thing to a friend I have right now and I'm keen to offload a little of this burden that's weighing me down.

The sun is still warm and the seagulls call out overhead, but otherwise all around us is silence. The perfect place to think and Freddie is the perfect companion to share it with, so as we walk side by side down the cobbled path toward the rickety gate that gives access to the beach, I take a few deep calming breaths and try to get myself together.

"So, why was the cop here?"

"Prepare yourself, Freddie, you are not going to believe this."

I begin to fill him in on what happened, and every word out of my mouth sounds far-fetched even to my own ears. By the time I've finished, we have reached our destination and stand looking at the sparkling sea that must be hiding a million rings on the sand underneath and Freddie exhales. "That's amazing, you must be happy you went."

"Yes, it was fun and opened my eyes a little. I mean, I've never been interested in history, or hearing about it, but now, after the day I've had, I have discovered there is a fascinating world that went before me that I'm keen to discover a little more about. For instance, the ring itself. I wonder who lost it, or did they place it there on purpose? How long has it been there and is there magic in it?"

Freddie starts to laugh and I nudge him sharply. "You may laugh Freddie Carlton, but I'm guessing there's a spell on it. Why did it literally fall into my hands and not anyone else's? It was meant for me; it was a sign."

He laughs and nudges me back. "Because probably no one else was dumb enough to scrabble around in the dirt praying for a husband."

"I did not."

"What scrabble around in the dirt, or pray for a husband?"

"Pray for a husband, of course. I don't need to pray for a man, Freddie, I came here to escape them."

Even though I was in fact praying for a husband and scrabbling around in the dirt, I don't want to come across as desperate and certainly not in front of a man who would probably laugh at that but to my surprise, Freddie's hand finds mine and he squeezes it hard and pulls me a little closer. For a moment, I'm so shocked I don't react and then he says sadly, "Maybe not, but isn't that what everyone wants, men included?"

"Maybe." I whisper and wait for him to speak because there's a sadness that surrounds him, making me wonder if he is nursing a broken heart inside that impossibly handsome exterior and that thought makes me a little sad for him.

Pulling me down beside him on the sand, we sit and watch the waves crash to the shore and he picks up a stone and skims the water with it. As we watch it jump a few times and then disappear, he says sadly, "I think everyone wishes for love at one point in their life. It's not natural to be alone. I would have probably done the same thing, in my head though. I doubt even I would actually crawl around in the dirt praying for love."

"You don't know that. I'm guessing you would still be there now until Saint Catherine offered you a signed contract and presented you with a vestal virgin that she plucked from within her history steeped walls."

He laughs softly, and I feel intrigued to discover why a man like Freddie is so sad.

"So, anyway, you have been doing a good job of searching for love yourself since you arrived. How was your, um, date?"

He turns and looks at me in surprise. "My date?"

"Yes," I swallow hard and try to look unconcerned as I shrug, "I take it you did meet a woman today, the barmaid perhaps?"

He looks confused, which surprises me a little. "You know, Freddie, that barmaid who served us yesterday, did you arrange to meet up today when I was in the, um, ladies?"

"What are you even talking about?" He laughs softly and then shakes his head. "No, I had the appointment arranged before I came."

"Appointment?" I stare at him in surprise, and he nods as

he looks out to sea. "Yes, if you must know, it was a business meeting. I could tell you about it, but then I would have to kill you, or at least ask Kevin to carry out the dirty deed on my behalf."

He grins and I push him so hard he falls onto the sand. Laughing, he rights himself and pushes me back and we engage in a war of shoving until the curiosity makes me say, "Can I ask what it was about?"

"I just said I couldn't tell you."

"I know, but that's made me want to know even more now. You could have just said it would be boring and wouldn't interest me, but you had to make it dramatic and now I'm intrigued."

He laughs again and then to my surprise, wraps his arm around my shoulder and pulls me close to his side and says wistfully. "If you must know all my secrets, I'll tell you, but you'll owe me one in return."

"I have no secrets."

I appear to be an accomplished liar in Happy Ever After because I don't even bat an eyelid as I stare at him with my innocent look and he leans closer and stares into my eyes and my heart thumps as it senses something shift between us. "Liar."

His lips hover so close, one false move and they would touch mine and despite every wall I've hastily built, I feel them crumbling inside in much the same way as the ones at Saint Catherine's Chapel, as I wait for some kind of magic to make all my dreams come true.

Then he pulls back and says casually, "It's no big mystery, really. For a while I've been bored, you know, looking for change. Life in Surrey isn't really shaping up how I wanted it to, so I started looking for a new project. My converted barn in Gomshall is now complete, and I put it on the market last month. Well, because I'm such an amazing designer, it was snapped up and now I'm house hunting and my search threw up an interesting proposition not too far away. The meeting was with an estate agent and we went through the details; I have a viewing tomorrow."

I open my mouth to speak, but no words appear because I was not expecting that.

"Why did you think I had a date?"

He turns and looks at me with a puzzled expression, and I shrug. "I suppose because you were flirting with the barmaid, I thought that's how you operate."

"Flirting! I was not."

"You were, actually. That's why she almost pushed me out of my seat and overstayed her welcome. Maybe you don't realise it but you are quite a flirt, you know."

"Maybe it takes one to know one."

"Excuse me."

"The police officer, you looked a little cosy when I turned the bend."

"We did not, anyway, you saw us for one second and we were definitely not cosy."

He nudges me again and I fall back a little and laugh. "Anyway, tell me about the property, it sounds interesting."

"I'll show you if you like, it would be good to have a second opinion."

"Really, I can come with you?"

"If you like."

He grins and as the breeze ruffles his hair and the sun catches his eye, I say, "Why do you find it so hard to find love Freddie, it should be easy for a man like you?"

For some reason, a shadow passes across his face and he looks shattered, making me regret even asking. He sits with his arms wrapping his knees and stares out to sea and says dully, "I'm not a nice man Susie and don't deserve to be happy."

"Don't be ridiculous, of course you do."

This time I put my arm on his and nudge him a little, trying to lighten the atmosphere that has changed suddenly. "Do you want to talk about it?"

"Not really, maybe, oh I don't know."

"Which is it?"

He shakes his head and then his mood switches in an instant and the lovable rogue is back in the room. "Anyway, I could murder a cup of complimentary tea, let's go and see if Sandra has any of that apple cake left and I'll show you my particulars."

He grins as he pulls me up from the sand and I roll my eyes. "You can keep your particulars under wraps, but the apple cake, now there's an offer I can't refuse."

It's only when we reach the little rickety gate, that I realise my hand is still in his and that shocks me a little because like Cinderella's glass slipper, it feels like the perfect fit. Is Freddie Carlton my happy ever after, or did the ring mean me to find the handsome officer? Or is there another man waiting in the wings with destiny stamped all over him? Maybe I will never know, or maybe all will become clear when PC Murphy does his investigations and tells me the story behind the ring.

CHAPTER 17

Once we're on the path walking towards our room, we hear a whisper from somewhere close. "Psst, over here."

Looking in the direction the voice is coming from, I see a strange sight. Lizzie appears to be sitting on a swing that has been strung up between two trees, and I stare at her in surprise. "Are you ok up there?"

We head her way and she grins mischievously. "I've been waiting for a strapping man to get me off."

Resisting the urge to laugh out loud, I say politely, "You mean to get you down."

"No dear, I mean what I say, I'm waiting for a man to get me off."

Freddie grasps my hand a little tighter and I don't know how I manage to keep a straight face, as he says faintly, "Would you like me to oblige?"

"Ooh, I was hoping it would be you. Or the ginger one from that fossil gang, what's his name again?"

"Noah?"

I stare at her in surprise and she winks. "Yes, Noah. I've

never had a ginger one before and if you believe the rumours, they say once you've had a ginge in your…"

"Anyway…"

"Freddie immediately interrupts the flow of conversation and I say with a giggle, "Anyway what, Freddie?"

He shakes his head and says in a clipped tone. "We should get you *down* before you fall *down*. Give me a hand, Susie."

We approach the swinging woman and her eyes light up as he reaches up and wraps his hands around her waist. I watch with amusement the gritty determination on his face as he pulls her effortlessly from her perch and sets her gently down on the ground. She wastes no time in wrapping her own arms around his neck and pulling him down to plant a huge kiss on his lips, which she doesn't appear to be in any hurry to pull away from. Freddie's arms flail helplessly at his side as she makes the most of the opportunity on offer until we hear a deep voice shout, "Unhand my wife, young man."

A man in military uniform pokes his walking stick in Freddie's back and Lizzie looks up and shakes her head. "What are you doing here?"

"Just patrolling the grounds and it's a good job because I am needed to defend your honour."

I look with interest at the man who must be the Major and see a very distinguished gentleman standing proudly nearby, but I don't miss the twinkle in his eye as he pretends to look shocked and disapproving.

Lizzie just rolls her eyes. "It's nothing you haven't seen before; I'll make it up to you later."

She releases a traumatised Freddie and dusts herself down before looking at me with interest. "I was hoping I'd run into you, young lady."

"Oh, why?"

I feel a little nervous as she looks at me with a considered expression and says lightly. "That ring you found, it's been on my mind since Sandra banished me to the wilderness, or in my case Kevin's man cave."

"I thought he banned you from there." The Major says in a deep voice and Lizzie shrugs. "As if I'd ever take any notice of him. Anyway, as I was rifling through his privates, it occurred to me that I could help."

"Really, how?"

I edge nearer, my interest pulling me to her with an invisible rope, and she grins. "Lolita Sharples."

"I'm sorry." I shake my head and look at Freddie in surprise and he just shrugs as Lizzie says with excitement. She's a fountain of wisdom, even if she is a little strange."

Once again, I share a look with Freddie because nobody is surely stranger than this woman.

"So, I gave her a call and told her you'd be around to visit. She said come around 10am because she likes to have an early morning swim in the sea to restore her powers."

"Her powers."

"Yes, dear." Lizzie lowers her voice. "Lolita is considered a white witch around these parts. What she doesn't know already, she learns from the spirits."

"What, ghosts?" I stare at her wide eyed and the Major snorts. "More like the alcoholic kind, the woman's fallen off more wagons than in the wild west."

Lizzie says angrily, "You know nothing about her powers, Major, she is a wise woman and we all know that clever people are one chromosome away from madness."

"Where does she live, can we walk there?" Freddie interrupts and Lizzie nods. "She lives in the bungalow in Love Lane. Turn right out of Happy Ever After and head down the hill to Love Lane."

Freddie is trying hard not to laugh and who can blame him. This place exists in a parallel universe and we are running to catch up with the crazy, so I just shrug and say with interest, "Does she have any information about the ring?"

"She told me she would search for it this evening. It will probably involve lots of alcohol and her tarot cards, but I'm sure she'll have everything you need by morning." She turns to the Major and winks. "Anyway, now Freddie got me off I need to get on again and you'll have to do. I think those boys are still out. Shall we try the one on the end? I don't think we've been in that one yet."

She throws Freddie a sly grin. "Would you care to join us, young man?"

He actually steps away and is luckily spared from answering when we hear a shocked, "Mother. I turn my back for one minute and you're out of control. The only place you're going is back to the McCarthy Stone if you carry on interfering with my guests. Now, come and help me inside, I've got a pile of ironing that should keep you busy for the next few hours and you…" She turns to the Major. "You can help Kevin with his logs. I will not have you wasting your days away when you can lend a hand here."

Lizzie heads off grumbling, closely followed by the Major and Sandra sighs. "I'm so sorry about them. To be honest, I don't know what to do about it all. No daughter should have to police her own mother, and especially not from being a predator. I'm so sorry, she's out of control and always has been."

As she turns to leave, I say quickly, "Sandra, do you know an, um, Lolita Sharples?"

"Yes dear, a little mad but harmless enough. Did Lizzie tell you about her, I wouldn't be surprised, they're nearly joined at the replacement hip."

"Yes, she told us she may know about the ring, do you think it would be ok to visit her for information?"

"Yes, darling, I'm sure it will. Just make sure to take her a little bottle of something, I think I have some homemade elderflower wine that would do the trick. If you take her alcohol, you are friends for life. She lives in Bluebell cottage on Love Lane. I'll sort out the bottle if you like, although word of warning, don't let her open it inside. It's best uncorked in the garden and remember to duck. It has a powerful release rate."

As she heads off, I stare after her in total shock and Freddie shivers. "That was close."

"What was?"

"Being tormented by that woman, I feel quite dirty."

"Why, because of the orgy invitation, or because of the mud on your trainers, they are seriously caked in it, you know."

He looks down and groans. "Great, these were brand new when I arrived. I'll have to clean them off somewhere unless…"

"No, clean your own smelly trainers, I'm going to grab that tea and cake and then settle down somewhere relaxing and finish my book."

We head back and there's a part of me that wishes he would hold my hand again. It felt so nice, as if we were a couple which reminds me how insane I am because finding a man this week was the furthest thing from my mind when I arrived and yet fate is literally throwing them in my direction, as well as a ring. It's a powerful message and I am now looking for love as if my life depended on it.

When will I ever learn?

CHAPTER 18

Later that evening Freddie persuaded me to accompany him to a sweet little pub that he drove past on his way back from his meeting, and as we walk inside the huge oak door, I look around with contentment. The warm white lighting creates a cosy atmosphere and the horse brasses that adorn the walls, mingle with the ancient farm implements that act as the finest art on the beamed walls. A fire flickers in the inglenook fireplace and the long polished wooden bar sparkles against a backdrop of every bottle of sprits going. As places to eat go, this is perfection and as we head to the bar, the lady that smiles her welcome makes me feel as if I'm with friends.

"Welcome to The Anchor Inn, have you booked?"

"Yes, Freddie Carlton, plus one."

"Susie, actually." I smile at the lady and she laughs softly. "Yes, plus one is a little impersonal, I like your style, anyway, what can I get you?"

"Susie?"

"Sorry we don't serve them here."

She laughs and I join her as Freddie groans and I say quickly, "A regular white wine would be lovely, thank you."

Freddie orders a pint of lager and we take our drinks, along with a couple of menus to sit in front of the flickering flames.

"This is nice."

"Yes, I thought so and the estate agent recommended the food."

I take a cursory look at the menu and before long a waitress stops by with a blackboard that she promptly sets on the table.

"Welcome, here are the specials, the soup of the day is chicken and the fish of the day is mackerel. The dessert of the day is spotted dick and the dish of the day is steak and ale pie. If you have any food allergies please let me know, and I would just like to say that our food is local and hasn't contributed to the destruction of the environment in getting here. We pride ourselves on our award winning food, as demonstrated by the one star rosette we display with pride on our entrance. If you need a potted history of the place, you can zap the Q code with your phone and prepare to be amazed. There are rooms available should you be in need of one and we have tea and coffee making facilities in all the rooms along with newly refurbished ensuites that…"

"Rose, a little help here."

The waitress stops in mid-sentence and looks over at the first lady behind the bar who flashes her a warning laden stare and she grumbles and says over her shoulder, "Any questions, I'll be back to answer them in just a minute."

Freddie raises his eyes. "Did you get all that?"

"Not really, I may need her to go over it again."

"Don't you dare, although the rooms sound interesting."

He winks and I colour up a little because it immediately

presents an image I can't seem to shake the more time I spend with him.

It doesn't take long before the waitress comes back and says somewhat sharply, "Are you ready to order?"

We decide on two steak and ale pies with a side order of garlic bread, and once again it strikes me that we like the same food. It's becoming a little weird now, but Freddie doesn't seem to think anything of it and settles back in his seat and sighs with contentment.

"This is more like it; I'm living the dream right now."

"Yes, it certainly feels that way."

He raises his glass to me and as they touch, I say with interest, "Have you spoken to Miles since you arrived?"

Once again, I see the guard go up and he shakes his head and says tightly, "No."

I try again. "It must be so nice to have a brother like him. I mean, he is perfect for Polly and seems a great guy."

"He is."

He looks into the flames and I sense he's brooding about something, so I say gently, "You look as if you have a lot on your mind, do you want to talk about it?"

"Not really."

He sighs heavily and says gruffly, "It's not a tale I want told, if I'm honest. I'd much rather hear about you, so tell me Susie Mahoney, why did your friend book you a trip to Happy Ever After, what's your story?"

Like him, I'm not keen to spill my dirty secrets and my hand shakes a little as I grip my glass tightly and take a gulp, before saying, "For a period of self-evaluation and grounding."

"You are mad."

"Takes one to know one."

We share a smile and I see uncertainty in his eyes that bothers me. It appears that Freddie Carlton is nursing a huge destructive secret that's tearing him up inside, and I'm keen to know what it is. The trouble is, I would be a hypocrite if I didn't practice what I preach, so I let my guard down a little.

"If you must know, I'm here to make a few life decisions because mine isn't really panning out how I thought it would."

He looks interested and I sigh. "The thing is, I've just broken off my engagement to a man I never loved in the first place, to escape one I thought I did. If you think that's confusing, it's only the tip of the iceberg."

"Sounds intriguing."

"I'll tell you some more if you tell me one of your secrets."

"Is that really how this is going to go?"

"Yes." I smile and fix him with a 'she means business' look, and he sighs. "Ok, I'm here because I have terrible taste in women and can't be trusted. Your turn."

"Is that it, not really the secret of the century, is it?"

"Well, I haven't got to that part yet and I doubt if I ever will."

"Why not?"

"Because like my brother, you would hate me and I'm not prepared to let that happen because quite frankly, Susie, I'm kind of enjoying spending time with you and want to weave my magic spell around your heart before you learn that I obviously haven't got one."

His words take me aback but before I can reply the waitress thumps a plate of garlic bread between us and says in a bored voice, "Here's your starter, do you need anything else?"

"Thank you, no."

Freddie smiles at her and for a moment I see her frostiness thaw a little and I die a little inside. Yes, Freddie is a heartbreaker, that's obvious, and I must proceed with caution.

The waitress heads off and I say lightly, "You think I'd

hate you; I doubt that for a second because I'm guessing you would hate me first."

"Why?"

"Because of what happened."

"Go on."

"Your turn."

"That wasn't much of a secret. Telling me you have one and it's bad isn't anything new. I need something more before I divulge one of mine."

Chewing on a piece of garlic bread, I look up in surprise as he whips a piece from my hand. "Forbidden, I like it, remember."

He pops the bread into his mouth and holds my eyes with his as he chews slowly, and I'm not sure if it's the fire or the man that's making me feel extremely hot right now.

Clearing my throat, I tear my eyes away from his and prepare to destroy his interest in me within seconds.

"I'm an escort."

"A what?"

"A woman who men pay to escort them to dinner, functions, dances, you know the sort of thing."

I see the spark in his eyes that usually accompanies my words, as men sense an easy time ahead and I say crossly, "I said escort, not prostitute, there's a difference you know."

"I never said anything."

"You thought it though."

"Who are you, the thought police now?"

"I saw it in your eyes."

"The only thing you saw in my eyes was interest. I've never met an escort before, and I'm guessing you have quite a few interesting tales to tell. Not really a big enough secret for me, I'm afraid, I'll need something way better than that before I give up mine."

He pinches a crust of bread from my plate and we share a

smile. I suppose I let my guard down a little by his reaction and say quickly, "I had an affair with a married man with a baby on the way."

He stops chewing and I feel the tears welling up in my eyes. "I didn't know he was married, though. I thought he was single and really liked me. I should have known really, I mean, he only met me during the day and only at my flat. We never went out, and I didn't meet his family or friends. The night I thought he was going to propose, I sent Polly off to meet Miles in my place and I pulled out all the stops. You know, candles, sexy undies and a gourmet meal…"

I break off and look down and he says softly, "And what happened next?"

"I was a fool." I raise my eyes expecting to see the disgust in his but all I see is sympathy, and he surprises me by reaching across and taking my hand.

"I'm sorry, Susie."

"For what?"

"For finding a man like that, you deserve better."

Once again, the waitress appears and clears away our plates and I feel a little awkward. What must he be thinking about me?

Once she leaves, Freddie says with interest. "What happened?"

"He offered to set me up in a flat, as his mistress I suppose. He didn't exactly word it like that, but I knew what he meant because he told me he wouldn't leave his wife and child until they didn't need him anymore."

"Ouch."

I nod and take another swig of my wine.

"Anyway, your turn."

"You can't leave it there; I want to know what happened next."

"After you."

He pulls a face which makes me laugh a little and he smiles. "That's better, you look so pretty when you smile."

"Thank you." For a moment we just stare into each other's eyes and I suppose reach an understanding. Freddie hasn't judged me by my profession and quite frankly disgusting past relationship, which makes me wonder about his own secret.

The food arrives, chasing away the opportune moment to ask, and it concentrates our minds for a bit on the job in hand.

It's only after a lot of polite conversation and a full stomach that he lets his guard slip a little.

"I almost went out with a married woman once."

"What do you mean almost, that doesn't count?"

"It does as it happens because she was engaged at the time to…" He breaks off and looks down as if he's struggling to get the words out. I find myself leaning forward and hold my breath as he whispers, "My brother."

CHAPTER 19

"Miles." I stare at him in shock, and he nods miserably.

"I told you it was bad."

"I'll be the judge of that when I hear the facts."

He half smiles. "Ok, if you insist."

Shifting a little on his seat, he fixes me with a lost expression and says gruffly. "I liked her from the moment I met her. Not in an attraction way, but as friends. She was good company, and we all got on fine. Kate was beautiful, witty and good company and I suppose I was a little jealous of Miles because he had found someone amazing and I was still trying. Anyway, to cut a long story short, we carried on just being friends until about six months later she arrived on my doorstep one night. It surprised me because she lived in Harpenden and I was in Guildford and it would have been a long journey but she seemed in distress, so I never thought about that."

"What happened next?"

"She told me she had broken it off with Miles, that she didn't love him and couldn't go through with it. I couldn't believe it and just held her; it was a natural reflex out of friendship because she was obviously devastated. Even then it didn't click and I just thought she needed someone to talk to and then she told me she couldn't get *me* out of her mind. Apparently, she had developed feelings for me and couldn't shake them. She tried every opportunity to arrange activities that included me and began to look forward to seeing me over my brother."

He looks so broken my heart goes out to him and I say gently, "That's not so terrible, you did nothing wrong."

"I slept with her, that night."

His words cut through the smoke from the fire and burn just as hot. "You. Slept. With. Her."

The words come out slowly, as if I need each one to register before the next one and he nods miserably.

"I couldn't fight my attraction and well, one thing led to another, and we ended up in my bed. The next day, I felt devastated by what we had done, but Kate was so happy, it rubbed off on me. She made it seem as if things would be ok and we would just have to give Miles time and he would come round."

"Did he, come round I mean?"

"No, he didn't. To be honest, it devastated my whole family. I'm not sure why, but I began to see things through Kate's eyes. They say love is blind, and that was certainly true of me. Miles was devastated, but I didn't see that. All I saw was her. My parents disapproved, and I fought it. My sister was disgusted with me and Miles. Well, I suppose it was the disappointment on his face every time we met that hurt the most. We stayed away from my family because it was too painful to see their feelings of hurt and betrayal. Kate moved in with me and I told myself I was happy because all I needed was her. It wasn't enough, you see, Suze, my family means everything to me. I hated being apart from them and it tore me up inside. I had destroyed something so precious for something that well..."

"Well, what?"

Reaching out, I take his hand in mine across the table and squeeze it reassuringly. "Well, it just wasn't worth it. Kate began to grate on my nerves. When I looked at her, I saw the woman responsible for destroying my life. We started to argue and I couldn't get past the fact I had betrayed my own brother. As it turned out, I mistook lust for love because I never loved her, not really, I know that now. You see, love is something that builds over time. It's woven into the fabric of our lives that takes years to grow and mature. What I had with her was infatuation, desire and as I said, lust. You can't build an empire in a few months, and I should know that more than most. It takes meticulous planning and an attention to detail, and what I had with my family was as important to me as my heart. I needed them to survive. Knowing that I had torn them apart broke me. I started to drink too much, became a man I hardly recognised and didn't like. I was ruined by a woman who had no business to."

"What happened?" He is retreating, I see it in his eyes as the disgust with himself returns and I watch as he stares into the flames with a haunted expression.

"As it turned out, Kate couldn't live with me because of the person I became. She left when I was at the gym and all I had to show for my betrayal was a letter and an empty heart. She wasn't worth it; I know that now and left me to pick up the shattered pieces and try to glue them back together. The trouble with that is that a once perfect object becomes tarnished. You can see the joins, the cracks that have been glued together, and that's how it is with my family. We go about the motions but the rough edges remind us that something once perfect is now hanging on by a thread and so I keep on trying to remedy that."

"How?"

"By trying desperately to find love to prove to them I am happy. I want to repair the damage and show them I have moved on and put this all behind me. Miles found Polly and is probably thanking me right now, but nothing will ever heal the rift my actions caused. The girls I have met and taken home have merely just reinforced my extremely poor judgement when it comes to women and it has done more harm than good, so I expect Miles sent me here to try to break the cycle."

"And you ended up here with me. A woman as broken as you, who makes the poorest decisions when it comes to men. What a pair we are, it's no wonder they staged an intervention."

We share a look that makes my heart flutter. When I look at Freddie, I understand him completely. Two identical souls who only really want one thing. Is it possible that Happy Ever After has woven its magic around our hearts, or are we just meant to help each other through a crisis and point one another in the right direction?

Once again, we are interrupted by the surly waitress who takes our dessert order and when she leaves, Freddie says with interest, "You say you were engaged. Tell me about that."

Thinking of Scott always makes me feel bad and I sigh. "He was a good man, *man* being the operative word. He was way older than me, and I met him through my job. I accompanied him to London one evening, and we had a really good time. He was attentive and made me feel special - he was good at that. I was in an extremely vulnerable state and Polly had just met Miles and wasn't around as much, so I dropped my guard a little and when he kissed me in the back of the taxi home, I let him."

I almost can't look at Freddie because this is probably

confirming his opinion of my job, so I say sadly, "I broke my own golden rule. I had sex with a client."

"In the cab?"

Freddie's eyes are wide and I laugh. "Of course not, idiot." We share a smile and if I thought he would be disgusted by that I was mistaken because all I see in his eyes is kindness as he says gently, "That's not so bad."

"It was worse, Freddie, you see, I used Scott to push away the pain of Kevin. He was rich, handsome and attentive. He seemed to really like me, and it was easy being with him. I told myself that was all I needed, but it wasn't. As it turns out, I need the whole package, and that includes love. I want to fall in love and not care how much money he has, what car he drives, or what house he lives in. I want to laugh, dance in the rain and make sweet memories. Scott would never allow the rain to dampen his designer suits. He would have an emergency umbrella somewhere and carry on with his day."

Suddenly, our desserts arrive and I'm glad of the interruption because talking about Scott leaves a bitter taste in my mouth and I need something sweet to counteract that. It's not because of anything he did either. It's because of the way I allowed myself to ruin his life because my own was in tatters.

Thinking of how I agreed to marry him, become a trophy wife and set up home in his huge house in Harpenden, makes me feel dirty inside. Just because he was so cold emotionally, it didn't mean he had no feelings at all. When I left, he looked more disappointed than devastated, which told me I had done the right thing. I suppose I was just another tick on his to do list because Scott lived for business and making money. I can't be with a man like that, I want energy and life in my future marriage that brings power to it. I don't want to merely go through the motions because that's what's expected of me.

Once again, Freddie pinches some of my cheesecake and it brings us back from the dark place we appear to have drifted to and I look at him in surprise. He stares at me with a hard expression and says gruffly, "Stop thinking on past mistakes, Suze. Leave them behind and move on."

"Says you."

He laughs and shakes his head. "Ok, let's make a pact."

"A pact, what is this, some weird public school club ritual?"

"No, it's a pact between friends who will be there for each other even when no one else is."

Why am I fixating on the word *friends*? If I feel a little disappointed, I push it aside and smile. "Ok, what do you have in mind?"

"When you need to talk, come to me and the same goes for me. Our past dies in those flames and we can only look forward. Think of our past mistakes as a pile of sand. Watch the waves come in and edge them away, leaving a blank, perfect surface to build castles on. That's us, Suze, a blank page waiting to be filled. No judgements, no regrets. Life begins here tonight and we owe it to ourselves to be happy. So, what do you say, no regrets, just hope for the future?"

He holds out his hand and as I take it, I wonder exactly what he means. Does he mean as friends, or something else? It's impossible to tell because he gives nothing away. Does he like me, fancy me, or just as friends? As we shake on it, I look for a sign but there is no lingering gaze, no heated lust filled expression, just compassion and friendship and my heart sinks. I shouldn't overthink things and just see what happens, after all, it's only been two days and a lot has happened.

Maybe friendship is the perfect base to build a castle on, only time will tell.

CHAPTER 20

When I wake the next morning, it's not to the sunlight breaking through the cracks in the curtains, it's to the sound of Freddie cursing as he stumbles against the bed.

"What's going on?"

I rub my eyes and sit upright, noticing him hopping on one leg as he tries to pull on his jogging bottoms.

"Sorry, Suze, I tried to be quiet but my balance could use some work."

"What are you doing?"

"Going for a run, do you want to join me?"

"Absolutely not." I stare at him in horror and he laughs. "Why not?"

"Because I don't run, Freddie. There is no possible reason in life to do so outside of an emergency. All it does it make you look on the verge of dying and for what gain?"

"Fitness, well-being and extending your life expectancy, perhaps."

He laughs softly and I roll my eyes. "More like bringing on a heart attack. No, I like to wake up naturally and allow my body to adjust *naturally*. A nice refreshing shower brings it alive and prepares me for the day ahead. Gentle relaxation is the key to happiness and sleep itself is the greatest medicine the human body can enjoy. It's why women mainly live longer than men because they know what's important and running around until your body is at the point of giving up on you, is *not* the answer. No, you will never catch me running for anything because there is absolutely nothing worth the torment involved."

"Don't you do any exercise then?"

"Occasionally I enjoy a game of tennis or a relaxing swim. I love walking, stretching exercises and a bit of meditation involving extreme yoga. That's as far as it goes with me. You see, I am more about exercising my mind than my body."

"Extreme yoga, sounds interesting, I love a woman of extremes."

He smirks and I shake my head. "You may mock, but I'm guessing you never tried it."

"Same goes for you, if you come running with me, I'll go extreme with you."

He grins and I laugh softly, "Good try but no. I'm snuggling back into bed and I'll think of you on your endurance test while I read a little. Maybe I'll have a pamper session and will arrive at breakfast refreshed and content after having nurtured my body, rather than broken it."

He just shrugs and grabs his headphones. "Your loss, I mean, it's the best part of the day. No one around, fresh air and nature are the best companions as you work up an appetite for the award winning breakfast in happy ever after. At least I will have burned off enough calories to make way for it and can eat without the guilt. Just saying."

"Good try my friend, but a brisk walk after breakfast will suffice and is probably the better option. No, you enjoy driving yourself to the brink, while I take care of my mind and body in a much more civilised way."

He shrugs and heads to the door and I admire the view for a little because Freddie Carlton provides a very fine one indeed. If I stopped to think how strange this is, I would be horrified. I have slept with a stranger twice now, although the barricade does help a lot. However, it doesn't feel wrong, something about it is right and I wonder what today will bring.

~

Now I'm awake, I decide to reward myself with that pamper I feel in dire need of. Luckily, I have brought the full experience with me and as I shrug on my fluffy white robe and slip my feet into the spa style slippers, I prepare for some alone time. This is what I thought I'd be enjoying here, not having to share with a man who has already complicated my luxurious stay and certainly not the added complication of the ring. Thinking of it makes me wonder if the woman we are about to visit may have some answers for me. I can't think that what she has to say will make any difference because that ring is probably lost to me forever because who doesn't report a Tiffany ring missing if they have any ounce of sanity in them?

As soon as I finish my luxurious shower with the special Victoria Secrets shower gel that was a present from some Christmas way back, I hear my phone buzzing away on the table beside the bed. It's a strange sound because up until now I haven't had a signal which has suited me just fine because I came to escape from my life, not bring it with me.

Seeing Polly's name flashing on the screen reminds me I have a few choice words to say to her, so I grab the phone and say briskly, "Polly, I do believe we used to be friends."

"Used to?" She laughs softly. "So, did you like my surprise, he's quite something, isn't he?"

"If you are referring to the unwelcome man in my bed, yes, it was quite a surprise."

"Really, in your bed already, wow, Suze, this has gone better than I dared hope for."

"Are you mad, he's only in my bed because you put him there and quite frankly Polly, I'm surprised at you. Why on earth did you think I'd be ok with sharing with a stranger on the mini break you arranged? We discussed my need to reconnect with my spiritual soul and I can't do that with him around."

"What are you talking about? I didn't book you in together, I didn't even book you in the same B&B, it was Miles who suggested it to Freddie when he told him he was heading that way on business. What's going on there?"

I sit down on the edge of the bed and stare at the floor in disbelief. "You mean, this wasn't arranged, and he was booked into his own room."

"Of course he was. What sort of friend do you think I am? Honestly, Suze, do you really think I'd expect you to share with a stranger?"

"But…"

"Suze, are you telling me that you and Freddie are booked into the same room?"

"Yes."

There's silence and then she says in a low voice, "I'm so sorry, I didn't know. When I booked the room, I made the booking in your name. There was no mention of Freddie, so I'm not sure what happened."

"Do you think Miles arranged it? I mean, Freddie didn't know anything about it either, he was quite shocked when I descended on him."

Polly groans. "Of course it was Miles, it's typical of him

and his family. They are always playing outrageous practical jokes on each other, but this is a step too far if you ask me."

"Polly…"

"Yes."

"Do you know anything about Miles and Freddie and their, um, relationship?"

She falls silent and I feel bad for asking, but after last night I'm keen to learn more. Suddenly, she sighs and I can picture her chewing her lip as she always does when she's stressed.

"Listen, Suze, Freddie made a bad decision and has been punishing himself for it ever since. Miles is worried about him; the whole family is because he appears lost. He's been wrapped up in guilt for too long now and when he told them he was thinking of moving to Dorset, it upset them."

"Yes, he did tell me what happened."

"He did? Wow, that's a breakthrough then because he doesn't speak about it even to his parents. What did he say?"

I feel a little bad gossiping about Freddie because from the sounds of it, it was in confidence, so I say brightly, "Just that something happened and he felt bad, anyway, what do you think of him? You're a good judge of character and I trust your judgement."

"Freddie is, well, utterly adorable. He is kind, funny and considerate and, as I said before, lost. He is trying to find something that should happen naturally and the string of bad decisions he made since, well, since his big mistake, would make your hair curl. Maybe he needs this break to regain his own spiritual soul. He has to do something because he is making things worse, not better."

As she speaks, I feel a sinking feeling inside. Freddie needs to heal, not to jump into another relationship. He needs time on his own, and maybe that's why fate threw us together. Two injured spirits in need of help. Perhaps friendship was always on the cards for us and I shouldn't look for something that isn't there.

Polly says softly, "What about you, has it helped to get away?"

"Oh, you know me, Polly, always taking a step into the unknown and falling deeper into mud the further I go. There is no such thing as an uncomplicated life where I'm concerned, and these last two days have reinforced the fact I should never be allowed out."

"Why, what's happened?"

"I'll tell you when I know. Anyway, I should get dressed because Freddie will be back soon and I don't want to be caught with no clothes on. Thanks for the call. At least it's repaired our friendship, if nothing else."

"Listen, Suze, I know you and you overthink everything. Whatever happened, happened, and now you must try to make the best of the situation. Take the time to rest and clear your mind and when you return, we'll work out where to go from here. You're not on your own, you know; you'll always have me."

"Thanks, Polly, I'll try to relax, thanks for the call."

As I cut the call, I stare at my phone, feeling troubled. Polly never booked us in together. Probably Miles did for a joke. Freddie is damaged and lost and needs to be left alone, much the same as me. Whatever secret I think the ring holds has absolutely nothing to do with me, and I should just put everything aside and concentrate on finding Susie Mahoney rather than making important life decisions.

With a strange detachment forming, I set about getting ready for another strange day and try to put all romantic thoughts out of my head. Romance is not my friend and never has been, so why did I think it would be any different in Happy Ever After?

CHAPTER 21

*L*olita Sharples lives in one of the prettiest cottages I think I have ever seen that sits at the end of Love Lane like a well-guarded secret.

Freddie stayed true to his word and accompanied me down the hill, armed with Sandra's bottle of elderflower wine and an interested smile.

"Not quite the image I had in mind."

He laughs as we stare at the little white cottage with a newly thatched roof. Beautiful pink roses drape all over the beamed covered porch and there is a delicious smell of baking wafting through the open window. The garden is well tended and I note with pleasure the white painted metal bench under the window, stuffed full of brightly coloured cushions offering respite for a weary traveller.

"I love it." I smile brightly as Freddie nods in agreement. "Me too. Dorset is the county that keeps on giving."

We watch with interest as the door opens and we see an older lady watching us with curiosity. She is nothing like I imagined, in fact, I'm not sure what I *did* imagine, but this lady is certainly no Lolita. She is smart in her Cath Kidston flowery dress with her grey hair pulled back with an Alice band. Her astonishingly blue eyes regard us with interest, and her red painted lips break into a smile when she sees the gifts we bear.

"You must be Susie and…"

"Freddie, ma'am." He steps forward and shakes her hand, and I register the approval on her face as she pumps it hard.

"I'm pleased to meet you both. I'm Lolita Sharples and you are very welcome."

Freddie hands her the bottle and her eyes gleam, which makes me want to laugh. The prim image of the woman before us is in direct contrast to the picture I formed in my head. I'm not sure why a name should conjure up an impression of someone, but hers definitely doesn't suit her.

She smiles, which completely lights up her face and she steps aside.

"Come in, I have some tea brewing on the Aga and have taken the liberty of making some currant buns to go with it."

As we pass her, I thank God I came here because I could move in permanently if she even hinted at needing a lodger. This place is definitely my dream become a reality.

Freddie has to stoop a little because the ceilings are low in a cottage that wouldn't look out of place in a fairy tale. Its chintz covered furnishings and polished wooden furniture are straight out of Country Living magazine.

Lolita says kindly, "Follow me, the best meetings are always conducted in the kitchen in my opinion, don't you agree?"

We nod and follow her through and it strikes me that we are both a little overwhelmed by Lolita and her heavenly home.

I'm not sure what I expected from Lizzie's description, but it certainly wasn't this. I thought she would be some kind of fortune teller, a gypsy perhaps; someone with a crystal ball and a cloth decorated darkened room, with a lamp with fringes on the shade. Not this country kitchen that smells so divine and makes me want to live here forever.

Freddie hops onto a bar stool with relief as he leans on the counter and eyes the buns greedily. Despite the fact we have just had breakfast, nothing will persuade me not to accept one of these if I'm offered one.

Lolita fetches some brightly coloured mugs from the cupboard and proceeds to pour some tea into them and says lightly, "I understand you found something of interest in St Catherine's Chapel. I must say, I was intrigued."

She slides the mug of tea towards me and I seize it gratefully. Then she pushes a plate of buns in my direction and if I have to fight Freddie for one, I would gladly do so. Happily, there are enough to go around, so as we sit eating, I fill her in on the events leading up to the discovery of the ring. By the time I finish, her eyes sparkle with interest.

"That's an amazing story. When Lizzie told me, I was intrigued and couldn't resist doing a little of my own investigation. I've lived here all my life and heard and seen many things but never anything as romantic as this."

She reaches out and takes my mug and I think she's about to refill it but instead she peers inside and then, to my surprise, turns it upside down and the remaining contents spill all over the work surface. Freddie catches my eye and the look in his makes me want to giggle, as she scratches her head and looks thoughtful.

"An interesting array of leaves, Susie."

"Really."

I look at the mess in astonishment and she peers a little closer. Then her hand reaches out and grabs mine and turns my palm to face her and she says in a low voice, "Fascinating."

Freddie is trying hard not to laugh, which annoys me a

little because it's obvious Lolita knows her stuff. She must do because who in their right mind does this sort of thing but she appears enthralled by my hand which piques my interest and I whisper, "What do you see?"

Freddie kicks me under cover of the breakfast bar and I glare at him as she says in a strange wispy light voice, "I see your future, my dear. The spirits are crowding you and shouting to be heard."

I feel a little uncomfortable about that and glance around me nervously. "What are they saying?"

"Quiet, I need to concentrate."

It feels strange being scrutinised with the afterlife as eager observers, as she nods and makes strange little sounds, almost as if she's talking in tongues. I am trying so hard to keep an open mind but am now wondering if her brain is riddled with alcohol because this is the strangest experience of my life. Freddie is polishing off another currant bun and trying not to laugh and I tune him out because I need to believe that Lolita Sharples is the real deal and I am about to learn my fate, making me squirm a little on my stool.

After a while she pulls back and looks directly at me, her cool blue eyes sharp and clear, and it's as if she is staring directly into my soul. Then she drops my hand quickly and reaches out and grabs Freddie's. He almost falls off his bar stool as she pulls him roughly towards her, and now it's my turn to stifle a laugh as he looks extremely shocked. She starts muttering again, and this time looks a little edgy, which makes me nervous. She is seeing something different in his hand and I wonder if that spells disappointment for me. I'm not sure why, but I had hoped she would have a potted history of the ring and its owner, not this show of fortune telling and spirituality.

By the time she drops his hand, the expectation hangs in

the air replacing the cosiness of before and as she looks at us with a little shock, I feel unease clawing at me inside.

"What did you see?"

She sits on her stool and shakes her head. "You have both led very colourful lives, it made for interesting reading. I saw deep pain, disappointment and uncertainty. You are both lost and seeking answers and it's no surprise the ring found you my dear."

She turns to Freddie and smiles sadly. "I'm sorry for your pain, you are struggling and trying to hide it. My advice would be to let go of the past and move on. You can't change what went before, but the future is very different. Don't be complacent and don't let the past define your future. You are about to be face the biggest challenge of your life and will need to remain focused."

"Um, ok."

Freddie looks completely out of his comfort zone, which ordinarily would make me want to laugh, but somehow, I believe every word this woman says and lean in eager for my own answers. "And me, what about my future? Do I get to keep the ring and who did it belong to?"

"The ring is yours; it was always yours, Susie."

"I don't understand."

"Destiny works in strange ways, and yours was always to find the ring. In the corner watching you is a woman who knows its secret. She won't come forward but is content to watch."

I look over my shoulder feeling extremely spooked right now, and Lolita looks in the corner of the room and nods mysteriously. "She is connected to this but won't say how."

Lolita looks at Freddie and frowns. "I'm not sure if she's here for Susie, or you young man, because there is an aura surrounding her of mystery. The connection is strong but is unclear. There is approval followed by anxiety. It's as if she is afraid of something and it concerns one of you, but it's unclear which one. Her spirit is unsettled, which may be why she won't approach; something is holding her back and I'm not sure what."

"Can't you ask her?"

I am so invested in this and firmly believe in Lolita's magical powers, and she shakes her head sadly. "No, the spirits must come forward voluntarily. It won't work any other way."

She looks up and smiles sadly. "She's gone, I'm sorry, we will never know."

"She may come back." I stare behind me hopefully and Lolita shakes her head. "I doubt I'll ever see her again. There is one message that came through loud and clear, though."

"Which is?" I think I hold my breath as Lolita smiles. "You will meet your destiny when you discover the story of the ring. Your life is tied up with that ring, my dear and it will take you down a path you never dreamed of."

"How will I find out about it, I'm due home in a few days?"

"The ring found you Susie and it will find you again. Believe in its power and don't close your eyes to any opportunity it presents."

I am feeling so frustrated and it must show because she smiles kindly. "We don't always see things clearly at first, but life has a habit of showing us the way when we most need it. It's not always obvious at first what that is, and sometimes things happen that we question that have a vital role to play in determining our future. Just go with it and enjoy the journey because from what I saw, you are about to travel an amazing one. At the end of it you will find happiness, of that I am certain."

"And you..." She looks at Freddie who is trying to look unaffected, but I see the uncertainty in his eyes as she smiles.

"Your decision will be the right one. Open your mind and don't be afraid of your feelings. You need to forgive yourself because until you do, the past will hold back your future."

She looks at the clock on her wall and sighs. "I'm sorry, I have run out of time. I'm due to my boxercise class in the village hall."

She laughs at our expressions. "You should try it, it's a fabulous way to let off steam and is one of the most satisfying classes that I teach. In fact, your delightful hostess Sandra is one of my regulars. I think she needs it more than most, poor woman, she deserves a medal dealing with her strange family and it's a good way to exorcize your demons."

Freddie smiles politely and says with a slight edge to his voice, "Um, thank you, it was very…"

He looks at me as if I am holding the words he seeks and I smile brightly, "Informative. It was very informative, Lolita and interesting. Yes, extremely interesting and, um, life changing. Also intriguing, did I mention that and surprising, yes..."

Before I can say another word, Freddie laughs and grabs my hand and smiles at Lolita politely. "Thank you. We'll let you know if we find anything."

"No need, dear..." She winks and laughs softly. "I have all the answers I need. Now, go and start that journey, it's an interesting one to be sure."

As we leave her heavenly home and begin the short walk up the hill, we do it in silence. That was the strangest morning of my life, and it's only when we reach the top that I realise that Freddie is still holding my hand.

CHAPTER 22

The first person we see when we walk down the path to Happy Ever After is Kevin, who appears to be pruning his roses. He looks up as we approach and smiles. "Just the person I was looking for."

He stops what he's doing and heads over and says quickly, "I've been doing a little digging into the ring and found something that may interest you."

"Really, what is it?"

"I trawled through the local history and there was one article I found that may tell us who it belonged to, if you like I'll tell you what I discovered."

"Yes, please." I make to follow him and Freddie says quickly, "I'm sorry, Susie, I must run because of the appointment. Did you still want to come with me?"

Now I'm torn because I really want to know what Kevin found, but I also want to go with Freddie. However, fate has another card up its sleeve and we look with surprise as a police car pulls up beside us and officer Murphy smiles as he winds the window down.

"Just the person I need to see."

I don't miss the twinkle in his eye and the slightly devilish smile he directs at me and I also don't miss that Freddie is looking a little worried right now, so I turn to him and say quickly, "Listen, I'm sorry, you should go to your appointment. Maybe it's best I stay here and sort out the ring, we'll catch up later."

He looks a little put out and smiles tightly, "Ok, no problem, until later then."

"Yes, oh and Freddie…" he turns and I smile. "Thanks for coming with me, I'm glad you were there to witness that."

"Yes, it was informative, as well as interesting, oh and exciting of course." he grins as I roll my eyes. "I get the message. Now go, you don't want to keep destiny waiting."

He turns and heads towards his car and for a fleeting moment, I feel like running after him but then officer Murphy brings me back to the matter in hand and says pleasantly, "So, I have some news that may interest you."

Kevin catches my eye and looks as interested as I am and the officer says quickly, "Maybe we should take a walk and I'll fill you in."

He stares at Kevin and says firmly, "If you don't mind, I'd like to talk to Susie alone, she may not want anyone else hearing what I'm about to tell her."

Kevin looks surprised, and now I'm intrigued. What has he found?

∽

Kevin leaves us and it feels a little strange to be alone with the officer who looks so official in his bullet-proof vest and black uniform. I'm not going to lie, it's not a bad look, rather gorgeous actually, and my voice reaches a high pitch as I clear my throat and say awkwardly, "So, what have you found?"

He smiles and my heart starts doing strange aerobics inside as he holds open the door of his police car and says mysteriously, "Let's take a little drive and I'll show you."

Ordinarily, I would never get in a car with strangers, but it appears that Happy Ever After is the exception to that. First it was the farmer's brother and now the rather gorgeous police officer and as I settle down in the passenger seat, I really hope he puts the sirens on.

He jumps in beside me and I swallow hard because I am struggling to breathe, being in an official car beside a man who must surely be most women's and some men's dream. As he starts the engine, he says loudly, "It's not far, I thought it would be best to conduct our business elsewhere."

Once again, he smiles and I grin like a love-struck schoolgirl and try to get my breathing under control as we speed through the narrow lanes where nature dominates rather than man.

On one side is the clear, sparkling sea and on the other, hills filled with sheep and cows. Officer Murphy says with interest, "So, how long are you staying in Dorset?"

"Just a few more days. I was booked in for a week and the time is passing quickly."

"It has a habit of doing that around here. So, what are you running home to?"

"Not a lot."

I smile sadly. "Life is pretty mundane really, but I'm working on that."

He nods. "I agree, it can get that way. So, are you here with your boyfriend, he must be happy that you found the ring, it could save him a lot of money in the future?"

He laughs softly and I say quickly, "Oh Freddie isn't my boyfriend, he's my best friend's boyfriend's brother but a stranger to me. We were booked into the same room by mistake. "I laugh self-consciously, "Strange coincidence, don't you think?"

"Are you serious, that must have been quite a shock."

"It was, but he's a nice guy and we get along, so no harm done."

"So, getting back to my earlier question, is there a boyfriend waiting for you back in Slipend, wasn't it?"

If I think his question's strange, I don't care because any form of attention from this man is welcome and I shake my head. "No, just a string of failed relationships and bad decisions litter the path behind me."

"I see."

I almost daren't ask, but grab the courage from somewhere. "What about you, is there a local girl who wishes she had found the ring on your behalf, or did you already make it down the aisle?"

"None of the above. This job is full on most of the time and very anti-social. My relationships have a habit of leading very short lives, but I'm fine with that because I believe in fate and not settling until you find your soulmate."

The distant crackle of voices on his radio fills in the silence as we speed along the deserted road, and I wonder where we're going.

Then, as we pull into a familiar side turning, I say with surprise, "You brought me back here – to the scene of the crime."

"It's the best place because you can show me where you found the ring. I'm mildly curious about that because in all my years in Dorset, I have never known anyone with such an amazing story as yours."

He comes to a stop on the track at the bottom of the hill and sighs. "It still involves a climb though, is that ok?"

"Of course."

I think I break all records in getting out of the car because walking anywhere with this man is an attractive thought and I'm just working out a way in which I can snap a photo of us to send Polly; she won't believe my luck.

As we begin the climb, I wonder what he has in mind.

CHAPTER 23

*S*aint Catherine's stands proudly against the backdrop to the sea and once again, I am overwhelmed with the whole experience. She is majestic, proud and imperious, and I wonder how many fair maidens of the past have made this pilgrimage. This time I am making it with a man who would be on most of their wish lists, and I feel extremely good about life right now.

We head inside and I look around the stone walls and wind swept interior and remember back to the last time I was here. Officer Murphy says with interest. "Can you show me where you discovered the ring?"

"Of course."

I head over to the door where I knelt in the dust and say anxiously, "Do I have to recreate it?"

He laughs softly. "Not unless you want to; it may be interesting to watch but not necessary."

He grins and once again my heart flutters because this man knows how to get a girl's pulse racing.

"It was here. I did what the women did in the past and put my hands and feet in the grooves. It sounds a little odd now, but at the time I was swept away by the history of the place and well, you know."

He starts to laugh and then heads across and stands beside me.

Now he's so close in the ancient monument, I think my whole body is on red alert because for some reason this feels so intimate.

He kneels down and runs his fingers through the dirt and shakes his head. "It's a miracle. I mean, to find anything in here at all would take some doing but a ring, and such a beautiful one, well, as I said, it's a miracle."

He looks up and my breath hitches as the sunlight catches the twinkle in his eye and they pull me in as he stares at me with a scorching look.

He holds my attention as he stands and turns to face me and to my surprise takes my hand. It seems a little odd to be standing in front of a very eligible man, on the very spot I prayed for one, and I am overwhelmed if I'm honest. Then he says huskily, "I did some digging of my own and discovered there is a legend attached to this ring."

"A legend." I gasp and he nods, his eyes simmering with something that almost mirrors lust. "I spoke to the local historian who told me that several years ago he heard a story that he dismissed at the time. A local woman was engaged to a man she was head over heels in love with. They were to be married and had a licence to use this very chapel. However, one week before the wedding, he was killed in a car accident and died outright."

Suddenly the ring has lost a little of its sparkle as my heart sinks. "The poor woman."

He nods and takes my hand and lifts it and then to my astonishment, removes a little box from his pocket and opens it, revealing the ring that I found. I stare in amazement as it sparkles in his hand and then blink as he slips the ring onto the third finger of my left hand and says huskily, "The historian told me that she was so desolate she vowed never to marry another because she would never be happy again. She wore the ring until she learned she didn't have long to live and decided to bury the ring in the very place they were to be married, in the hope that one day it would join two people together. She trusted Saint Catherine to find the rightful successor to the ring, and the historian told me she believed that whoever found the ring while they prayed for a man, would find her true love the very same day. She firmly believed that Saint Catherine would make the right choice and the wearer of the ring would live happily ever after with the first man she met since finding the ring."

I stare in amazement as he lifts my hand and whispers, "What do you say, Susie, do you believe in fate?"

I gaze into his deep brown eyes that are staring at me with a longing that mirrors my own and he leans closer and whispers, "So, the ring is rightfully yours, but what about the man? Who was the first stranger you met, who Saint Catherine has chosen for you?"

My mind is scrambled as I look into his eyes and all around me the sound of seagulls crying and sheep bleating punch through the silence. A slight breeze ruffles my hair and I feel a shiver pass through me as I stare into the officer's eyes.

He leans closer and his lips are just centimetres away as he whispers, "As I said before, do you believe in fate, Susie, because I do. I believe that it was no chance find, it was always meant to happen. You were destined to find me that day, and I haven't stopped thinking about you since we met. Ring aside, I felt it the moment I first met you, did you feel the same?"

I am so caught up in the moment, I don't even question my sanity as I nod slowly, "I think I did."

He kisses my hand and says gently, "Then we owe it to Saint Catherine and the poor woman who placed it there to at least see if there's anything in the legend. Would you do me the honour of meeting me later for dinner? I would love to get to know you more, if you want to that is."

"Of course, thank you."

I don't think I've ever been in such a romantic position in my life, and I am totally carried away with it. The legend must be right. Alex Murphy was the first stranger I met that day since finding the ring. If it hadn't been for the ring, I would never have met him, and if he hadn't been on duty, it wouldn't be him. Fate has delivered my happy ever after to me, as I hoped it would in such a magnificent way. Of course, I need to explore my options because quite frankly I'm a bit short of them right now, so I nod and say nervously, "I'd like that."

I almost think he's going to kiss me, but instead, he laces his fingers in mine and kisses them, before kissing the ring, reminding me how special this is.

"Come, I'll take you back and then I'll head to the station and finish my shift. I'll pick you up at seven, and Susie…"

"Yes."

"I think this date could change both our lives."

As I follow him out into the bright sunshine, I'm in absolutely no doubt about that.

CHAPTER 24

I feel so conflicted and as Alex, as he now insists on me calling him, drops me off with the promise of a hot date later, I head towards the pretty cottage of happy ever after feeling like a different woman. How has my life changed so quickly? It's as if I'm living in a parallel universe and ordinary life has been replaced by the extreme. The ring feels heavy on my finger and far from feeling happy and excited, I just feel so worried right now and the first person I see heading towards me carrying a trug filled with freshly picked flowers, is Sandra.

She smiles broadly and stops for a chat.

"Isn't it a lovely day, you should go for a walk by the sea, so invigorating."

"Um, maybe."

She must sense my inner turmoil because she peers a little closer and then says briskly, "I've just baked some honey bread. Would you try some and let me know what you think, it would be so helpful?"

She smiles and I can't agree quickly enough.

"That would be great, thank you."

"So, I see you got the ring back, or is that another one you found while taking a morning stroll?"

She laughs lightly and I smile. "No, it's the same one. Alex gave it back to me. Apparently, the owner has died and always meant for it to be found."

"Alex?"

I must blush a little because she looks interested. "I can see a lot has happened. Would you like a friendly ear to offload to?"

"Would you mind? I mean, to be honest, Sandra, my head is spinning with it all right now."

"Of course, come inside and I'll fix a pot of tea and you can fill me in over the honey bread."

∽

Sandra's kitchen is much like the woman herself. Welcoming, open, friendly and comforting. As I sit in the rocking chair by the fire, I really do think she has it all. Timmy is snoring peacefully in his bed by the Aga, and all around me is the scene of perfect domestic bliss.

As she hands me a mug of steaming tea, I accept it gratefully and my mouth waters at the scent of honey bread wafting towards me as she cuts me a slice.

"So, what did Alex say?"

Once again, the ring sparkles as it catches the light and I feel so conflicted.

I fill her in on the story and Sandra looks interested. "Yes, Kevin did tell me a similar one this morning. He was up late last night researching it."

"Oh, I'm sorry…"

She waves her hand. "Don't be sorry, dear, it did me a favour actually. Kevin's snoring is out of control and it enabled me to get to sleep before he came to bed. Anyway, I know him and when he gets a bee in his bonnet about something, he won't rest until he's sorted the problem."

"What did he find?"

"The same as the dashing officer, I think, although his version was a lot less romantic. What are you thinking right now, you must be a little confused, I know I would be?"

"What would you do?"

"About what? I mean, on the one hand, some may think you've landed the jackpot. A valuable ring and a rather handsome suitor all in the same day. What's not to be happy about, unless…"

"Unless what?"

"Unless you're pining after a different suitor. Maybe you had hoped for someone else, a certain roommate that has created rather a stir around here."

"What, Freddie?" I shake my head rather too quickly and shiver. "I don't think he's my happy ever after, Sandra. Freddie is too…well, gorgeous to be the real deal. I mean, I know that sounds mad, but he is. I would be always looking over my shoulder, wondering if he's about to run off with the next girl who falls at his feet."

"And you trust Alex, if you ask me, he's not much different."

"Possibly, but what am I to do? The legend has spoken, and I have met my match. In fact, he has come as a package with the ring. Surely that's all the reassurance I need and he does seem nice."

"Are you sure about that?"

"About what?"

Her voice lowers and for the first time since I met her, Sandra looks worried. "Listen, don't be fooled by the legend. You only have Alex's word on that and well, some men will say anything to get a pretty girl. My advice would be to keep your options open. Don't rush head first into a situation before knowing the facts first. If it's meant to be, it will be. Take some time and see what happens, you don't have to make any decisions."

"But I leave in a few days' time. I don't have the luxury of time, it's an impossible situation."

Sandra looks thoughtful. "So, if you went home, how would you keep a relationship going with Alex?"

"Oh, I don't know, Sandra, I haven't thought that far ahead. I mean, who's saying there *will* be a relationship? I've just met the guy; I haven't had time to work out the details."

She nods with approval. "Then just enjoy your stay and go home at the end of it and see what happens. As far as I can see, you don't have to make any decisions, anyway. You're a lucky girl really, I wish I had your dilemma."

The door opens and we look up and I see Lizzie and the Major heading inside, looking a little out of breath. Lizzie's cheeks are flushed and her breathing erratic and Sandra winces as she says with a hint of disapproval, "I'm not going to even ask what you've been up to, come and sit down and I'll fix you both a cup of tea."

She jumps up and Lizzie almost falls into her vacated chair as the Major perches stiffly on another. "Thanks, you're a life saver."

Lizzie fans her face and says disagreeably, "I told you it was too far, but no, the Major knows best, he's been in the army and can read a map." She scoffs and throws him an angry look before turning to me and saying loudly, "I think he wants to finish me off so he can shack up with Elsie Masters. What was meant to be a gentle stroll turned into an ordeal, a walk of extremes against the harshest elements. My heart nearly gave out three times and my legs will take a week to recover. I'm not sure if I even have legs anymore because I can no longer feel them. Honestly, Major, you should brush up on your skills at how to give a girl a good time and just for the record, power walking to the post office is not one of them."

"Power walking." Sandra stifles a grin as she hands her mother a mug of tea and the Major says with resignation, "I thought you'd be ok, I mean, it's only down the hill."

"Down the hill was fine, it was the getting up part that was a problem."

"Yes, well, I never have that problem." He winks at her and she giggles, which makes me feel a little hot under the collar. Sandra looks as if she has a bad taste in her mouth and Lizzie just stares at the Major with a soft look that shuts the whole world out. As I look at them, I see true love right in front of my eyes. Two people who refuse to let their age dictate their lives and carry on like teenagers, in their mind, anyway. I really hope I'm like them and find the one who keeps me young at heart like they obviously are.

Lizzie turns to me and says with interest, "I saw Lolita in the post office, she mentioned you'd visited. I must say, it all sounds intriguing, you're a lucky girl."

"I am, of course, but with great riches comes great responsibility and I'm not sure what to do if I'm honest."

Lizzie shrugs. "Do whatever, or whoever, comes your way if you want my opinion."

"We don't." Sandra's voice is sharp and loaded with warning, but Lizzie shrugs it off. "Lolita told me that ring holds the key to your future. You can't argue with destiny, my girl. Look at me and the Major. Fate delivered him to me, and if I hadn't put out on the first date, I wouldn't have held his interest. Sometimes in life you have to take risks and some of them actually pay off. I mean, when I met Sandra's father he was already married."

I feel a little uncomfortable as I anticipate a skeleton jumping out of Sandra's closet, who looks less than happy at the mention of her father.

"Turns out his wife had left him for his best friend, so it all ended up happily for me. He was on the rebound and I couldn't get my claws into him fast enough. Well, one woman's scandal is another's gain, and we were very happy for many years until he died."

I feel bad as she wipes a tear from her eyes and sniffs, "He was a good man right up until the point he died. I was so happy with him and it has taken an exceptional man to fill his boots."

She blows a kiss to the Major who stares at her fondly. "Yes, his death is my gain, I should thank him for that."

Sandra looks as if words have failed her and Lizzie nods. "Yes, it was lucky for you he died because I would never have looked at you twice if he had still been around. Anyway, as I said, fate works its magic in mysterious ways, Susie and I'm guessing your fate will take a few surprising twists and turns before it's done with you."

The conversation switches rather skilfully on Sandra's part to more general topics, and when I leave their company, I feel a little bit of calm descend on me as I walk along the cobbled path to my room. Maybe I should just go with the flow and see what happens. Sandra's right, I don't have to make any life choices by the time I go home, *if* I go home, because the thought of leaving Happy Ever After is not a happy one.

CHAPTER 25

Freddie still isn't back, and I feel a little bad about leaving him to go to his appointment alone when I said I'd go with him. I'm not sure what to do to fill in the time before Alex returns at seven, and so I decide to act on Sandra's advice and go for a walk along the beach. It's a lovely day and it would be a shame to waste it, so I set off feeling quite glad I'm on my own. That's why it surprises me to see the man and woman from dinner walking towards me hand in hand, looking quite animated. She even smiles as she approaches and stops for a chat.

"Beautiful day, isn't it?"

"Yes, lovely."

The man smiles sweetly. "I'm Greg and my wife is Eloise."

"Susie." I smile and Eloise grins. "We heard about your find, it's all anyone can talk about and I must say, it's really captured our imagination. Greg has ordered a metal detector from Amazon, which should be there when we return home. We're thinking of making it our new hobby."

He nods. "It will be good to have a shared interest and if I'm honest, we have you to thank for that."

"Me."

Eloise nods and says almost shyly, "I don't know, watching you and that lovely companion of yours, reminded me of how we were when we first met. Years of marriage and normal life has made us lose sight of what we once had and as they say, familiarity breeds contempt. Well, seeing you run at life, full speed ahead having an amazing adventure, made us both think and now we are determined to recapture the spirit that appears to have fallen by the wayside as life got in the way."

Greg nods and squeezes his wife's hand. "Yes, I'm to blame for that more than most because I work and there's not much room for anything else. I suppose I neglected Eloise a bit and we are more like strangers than lovers."

He stares at his wife and smiles. "Coming here to Happy Ever After was a shot at spending some time together without all the stresses of normal life. It seems to have worked because we have fallen in love all over again and our new hobby is a good way of making time for each other."

"What we want to say is, thank you for opening our eyes and showing us that it's ok to step outside your comfort zone because what's there is far more exciting."

I'm not sure what to say because I haven't done anything, certainly not anything that warrants such praise, and I feel like a charlatan.

Instead, I just smile and say happily, "I'm glad things are working out well for you."

Eloise nods and then says with excitement. "Well, we've been talking and think you should approach the local news with your story. I mean, this is a fantastic find and I'm pretty sure it will capture people's imaginations. They will want to follow your progress and Greg knows a thing or two about media because he's a reporter for the Daily Telegraph."

Greg nods. "I would love to do a piece on it, take some

pictures maybe, document the whole story and give hope to those struggling to find love everywhere."

"A piece on me, really?"

I'm not sure why that thought fills me with horror, probably because I've always been quite a private person, mainly out of embarrassment at my job and the thought of strangers delving into my life is not a pleasant one, so I shake my head and laugh a little self-consciously. "Oh, I don't know, I'm not one for publicity."

Greg hands me his card. "Listen, think about it, and if you change your mind, give me a call. You never know, it may lead to some amazing opportunities for you, don't dismiss it out of hand."

My fingers close around the small piece of cardboard and I wonder what would happen if I took Greg up on his offer. Would I become a media celebrity with people keen to follow my Instagram in the hope of seeing pictures of me with my one true love and ring? Maybe I should use this opportunity and take some pictures at the chapel and really milk this whole unbelievable situation. Then again, I just want to run back to my shared room and bury my head in the scatter cushions because my life is unravelling fast and I'm not keeping up.

The couple leave and I carry on walking, looking for answers on the sand below my feet. Deciding there isn't any, I try the next best thing and dial Polly's number.

"Hey, Suze, how's it going in Happy Ever After?"

I fill her in and she sounds shocked.

"A date with an officer and from the sounds of it, a gentleman. I never saw that one coming. How do you feel about that and what about Freddie?"

"What about Freddie, to be honest, Polly, there was no Freddie in my life until you interfered so spectacularly?"

"Oh, about that."

"What?" My heart is beating fast as I wait for another bomb to explode at my feet and she sighs.

"It tuns out it was Pauline who made the call to book you in the same room."

"Pauline! Who's Pauline?"

"Freddie's mum. You know, I've spoken about her before. She's amazing if I haven't already told you that, and I've always thought you two would have loads in common. I mean, she loves crafting and decorating presents and we both know you could teach a course on that. She's also a little wild and unpredictable and not afraid to go after what she wants."

"But why would she book her son into the same room as a stranger, she doesn't even know me? I could be a sex pest or something."

"I think that's what she was hoping for."

"Polly!"

I'm scandalised and Polly laughs, then says more seriously. "Actually, I think she'll try anything right now. Freddie worries her because all she wants is for him to be happy. The last few girls he's brought home have upset her, and she is despairing that he will ever find happiness. I've spoken a lot about you and told her you would be perfect for one another and when she saw your photograph, she said you were just his type and got quite excited."

"Then you obviously didn't tell her what I do for a living, I bet she wouldn't be so keen then."

"On the contrary, she knows that's how I met Miles and I've assured her it's all perfectly respectable and not a bad way to earn a living."

"You've changed your tune. I thought you disapproved of my occupation."

"I'm not going to lie, I did, until I experienced it firsthand. No, Suze, you have nothing to be ashamed about and are a good person who deserves a little bit of luck. The fact it appears to be descending on you like a tsunami can only be a good thing, can't it? I mean, a girl likes to have choices and yours, by the sounds of it, aren't difficult ones to live with whatever you decide."

"But what if I choose Alex and decide to emigrate to Dorset?"

She laughs softly, "Dorset isn't a foreign country, it's just a day away. Anyway, how do you know Freddie isn't emigrating himself, I believe he's looking at property there, which is why he was heading that way in the first place? As is usual for most men, he left it to his mother to arrange the finer details and as Pauline is a little wily herself when it comes to manipulating affairs of the heart, she came up with what she thought was a fool proof plan. I don't think she expected your brush with Saint Catherine though, so it's now up to you to decide where your heart lies. With Freddie, with Alex, or back in Slipend with your normal life."

I think about her words and feel more confused than ever. "So, just say I did decide to relocate, I doubt I'd find much work as an escort down here. What would I do, I can't live on fresh air, you know?"

"Details, details, it would all work out in the end. Anyway, I should go because I was due in a meeting ten minutes ago and it won't make me look good. Chin up, Suze, you'll make the right decision in the end, you will just make a song and dance of it along the way."

Her laughter is the only sound I hear as she cuts the call, and a lone seagull regards me with interest as I stare at the nearby cliff wall. "It's all right for you, you don't have life-changing decisions to make, just where to fly to next."

"Talking to yourself is the first sign of madness, then again, nothing surprises me where you're concerned."

With a start, I jump and look around and see Freddie staring at me with a smirk. "Where did you come from?"

"Hell, Susie, pure and utter Hell."

He rakes his fingers through his hair that makes me question every decision I will ever make in life and shakes his head. "That uptight couple told me they'd just seen you when I came looking. I really could use someone insane to distract me from the morning I've had."

"Don't you mean sane?"

"I mean what I say." He laughs, and despite the fact I am glowering at him with my perfected death stare, I am fully aware I'm happy to see him. Maybe it's because he has become familiar over the past few days, or maybe it's because I am thinking of him more and more as the hours pass. Freddie Carlton appears to be the first person I look for, and I expect it's because we're so similar. Maybe that's why I feel so comfortable around him, it's because I get him, I understand how his mind works because apparently it works in much the same way as mine.

CHAPTER 26

We carry on walking while Freddie tells me about his hellish morning.

"You know, Suze, the place was amazing, better than it looked on the internet. They got that right and ordinarily I would have made them an offer on the spot."

"Then why didn't you?"

"Because it was a wreck, uninhabitable and almost falling down."

"Hmm, I can see that would be a problem." I laugh as he shakes his head.

"I couldn't even go inside."

"Why, didn't you have a hard hat and high viz jacket to hand?" I nudge him and he shivers. "Actually, I do, it's the usual kit that I keep in my car for site visits. No, the problem was with the inhabitants."

"I thought you said it was inhabitable."

"It is but we are not talking about humans here."

"What, aliens?"

My eyes are wide and he shivers. "Worse, spiders."

"Oh my god, no way. I can see why you had a problem.

Were they giant man-eating ones, or those deadly poisonous ones that crawl into your shoes when you're not looking and sink their venom in your ankle when you least expect it, resulting in a mad dash to A&E for the antidote?"

He nods and for a moment I am right there with him in hell as he put it.

Then he shakes his head and whispers, "It was awful, Monica couldn't understand my reluctance to go inside. She was literally 2cm from one, and I could only focus on that. It was as if I had lost the power of speech and couldn't form words. Instead, I just pretended I had seen enough and made another appointment to bring my friend along next time."

"Your friend."

"Yes, you."

"No Freddie, that's a step too far. Why are you sacrificing me to gain access to the arachnahouse? I won't be used as a human shield that way."

"Well, hopefully I have the answer to that."

"Which is."

"Lizzie."

"You can't use an old woman either, it's not moral or decent or right on any misguided level. Anyway, it won't be safe for her. What if a wall crumbles on top of her, or she falls through the rotten floorboards? You would have her death on your conscience."

"It won't come to that, it's not that bad."

"How do you know; you never went in?"

"Because I just do, so, will you come with me tomorrow morning and can I leave it with you to arrange our chaperone? I would, but that woman scares me."

I feel a little bad because of Alex and feel as if I owe him this at least, so I nod. "Ok, but I'm going in after you and Lizzie. I'm not sure how much help I'll be though, it appears that I can't make a decision to save my life these days."

"What's happened then?"

I feel a little reluctant to tell him about Alex and the ring wearing incident and try to brush it off. "Well, Alex, you know the police officer dealing with my case, took me back there today."

He looks interested. "The scene of the crime."

"Yes." My heart sinks because as always, he thinks along the same lines as me and I sigh. "The thing is, Alex told me the ring is mine because it was always intended to be found by a deserving singleton."

"And that's you." He grins and I shrug. "Apparently so. It would appear that a woman buried it there when her own fiancé died and she never met anyone else. She entrusted her ring to Saint Catherine to join two more lost souls together and give them everlasting love.

"I see."

My heart sinks because I doubt he's seen coming what happened next, so I take a deep breath and say weakly, "Alex thinks it's him."

"What?" Freddie looks puzzled and I laugh nervously. "He told me about a legend attached to the ring. Apparently, whoever finds the ring will meet her true love immediately afterwards. The first, um, single stranger she meets after finding it - is the one. Well, that one was Alex, and he seems keen to investigate things further."

"Well, I suppose he is a police officer, it's what they do."

"No, Freddie, I mean, he is keen to investigate the legend further – with me, him, with an um, date."

Freddie looks shocked and I see a hint of disappointment in his eyes as he says tightly, "I see. And what do you think of it?"

"I'm not sure what to think. The whole thing is getting more surreal as the days go by. I can't forget Lolita's words either, you know when she said to seize any opportunity the ring presents. I must at least go out on a date with him, don't you think?"

"Of course, yes, but…"

"But what, Freddie?"

"Oh nothing, you're right, you should seize every opportunity and it sounds as if this could be what you came here for."

"I suppose."

Once again, I feel bad because as soon as I told Freddie where I was going, the atmosphere changed. It feels a little awkward now and I can tell he's not happy, which makes me feel as if I'm betraying him somehow. I'm not sure why because we are just stranger friends, nothing more, nothing less, but we share a soul. I can feel it and it's as if I know what he's thinking and I suppose what I mean is, I know Freddie Carlton because he is the mirror image of me.

We decide to walk back to the house and conversation is a little more stilted. I don't want to talk about Alex and try to learn a little more about the house, but Freddie has shut down, and no longer seems interested in that subject. As we near the gate leading to the cobbled path leading back to the room, I say almost apologetically, "What will you do this evening?"

He shrugs. "I'm not sure. I saw the guys earlier, and they said if we were at a loose end, they were hitting the local pub. I may take them up on their offer."

Picturing the buxom barmaid who will no doubt be ecstatic to see Freddie again, I am surprised by the surge of jealousy that flares inside when I think of him spending time in her company.

There's nothing I can do about that, so I try to push it aside and concentrate on my own evening ahead and wonder what it will bring.

CHAPTER 27

Alex is looking amazing in black jeans and a black leather jacket. He is leaning against a shiny red sports car and throws me a lazy grin as I totter over to him on my stilettos, holding my coat firmly around me. The weather may be warming up in the day but the nights are still cold and despite the fact I agonised over what to wear, I have made it look as if I just threw the outfit on without a care. I'm wearing a wraparound dress and my excruciatingly painful shoes. I have curled my hair and spent thirty minutes on my make-up, and I'm feeling quite good about how I look. The ring is flashing on my finger but I have moved it to the other hand because after all, I'm not engaged yet and don't want to presume anything.

Alex smiles and holds open the passenger door like a true gentleman, and as I sink into the leather seat, I congratulate myself on landing such a prize. Alex is surely every girl's dream. Good looking, charming, attentive, has a good job and great taste in cars. I'm looking forward to spending some time with him and as he joins me and starts the engine, I lean back, feeling the butterflies inside as I wonder what the night will bring.

"So, have you thought about the ring and the legend since I told you?"

We crawl out of the driveway and I shake my head. "I have, but decided to just go with the flow. I don't think you can force true love, so I'm keeping an open mind and trying not to let the romance of the situation carry me away."

"Good idea, that's what I thought."

"Really."

He grins and says slightly huskily, "Ring aside, Susie, I was interested from the moment I saw you. It may sound strange, but there was something about you that made me think we had met before. I struggled a little with it because I thought it was odd at the time, but when I saw you again, it came back."

"Oh." I'm not sure what to say, and Alex laughs softly. "When I slipped that ring on your finger, it just felt right. I must just say I don't have a habit of propositioning all the women I come across, but I was aware I didn't have long. You're leaving soon, and when the local guy told me about the story of the ring, it just told me I was right. *We* are right and I don't need the ring, or the story, to know in my heart I want to get to know you better."

Swallowing hard, I stare out of the window at the day making way for night and wonder how to answer him. It's a bit full on if I'm honest, but I do understand what he's saying. We don't have long and if he feels something, then who am I to judge? He is certainly a good catch, and I would be a fool not to act upon my attraction to him. Then there's the ring. I can't ignore what it's telling me, so I smile brightly and nod. "Yes, we don't have long, so we must make the most of the time we have."

"So, tell me about you and your life in Slipend. What do you do for a living?"

I think I hold my breath as I throw the first test right out there.

"I'm an escort."

For a moment, there's silence and then he says in amazement, "An escort as in…"

"In escorting paying customers to events as their date. A little unconventional I know and not anything illegal, or sordid, just a paid for companion."

"I see."

Once again, the silence settles between us and I feel judged. I'm pretty certain the opinion Alex had of me has sunk a bit lower and it makes me feel a little worthless. Then, to my surprise, he reaches out and laces his fingers with mine and says softly, "It sounds like a fun thing to do, much better than my own profession, which is quite damaging to the soul if I'm honest."

I stare at him in surprise and he smiles, making the ice thaw a little in my heart.

"It's not much fun dealing with people who are in trouble or breaking the law. Being the first on a crime scene takes a lot of getting used to and its hard having to explain every decision I make and the repercussions make for a very unrelaxed form of living. It's difficult to meet anyone because I'm always on shift and when I'm off, everyone else is at work. I've tried the usual dating sites but as soon as they learn what I do for a living, the shutters come down and they seem worried half the time in case I'm going to arrest them for an unpaid parking ticket or something. It's not just the women I meet, it's their families too. Always guarded around me and not keen to chat for fear of recriminations. It's quite a lonely life really, so I'm guessing being paid to go out and eat, in return for polite conversation is as good as any way to make a living."

"Yes, it is." My voice softens because Alex is tearing down my emotional walls and leaving me feeling surprised. He's different to how I imagined. More approachable, less official, and underneath that uniform is a regular guy, much like those I meet on a daily basis.

He carries on. "So, would you ever consider relocating if you did find the man of your dreams – just asking for a friend?"

He laughs and I can't help but join him. Alex is charming, witty and seriously gorgeous, and suddenly I'm interested way more than I was before.

I'm spared from answering his question as we pull up outside a restaurant in the nearby town and I see, Haddon House Hotel, illuminated in lights before me.

"This looks nice."

Alex nods. "I didn't want to take you to a pub. I thought I should be a bit classier than that, and this was the first one that came to mind."

He opens my door and helps me out, and it all feels a little surreal. The handsome companion, the sports car and the Tiffany ring are acting like a drug on my emotions as I fall under his spell. As he guides me towards the door with his hand low on my back, I don't mind it there at all. It feels nice actually, and I am looking forward to an interesting evening.

We are greeted by a waiter who shows us to a table overlooking a beautiful garden, and Alex smiles sweetly. "What would you like to drink? I could order a bottle of wine, but I'm afraid I can't drink and drive."

"Of course. No, a glass would be fine, I'm not a big drinker."

Alex orders a white wine for me and a soda water for himself and stares at the menu.

"It all looks good, what were you thinking of?"

"The seafood medley looks nice."

"Ok, do you want a starter?"

"Not really, do you?"

"I wouldn't mind the pate, followed by the lamb shanks. I'm not a lover of seafood, weird when I live by the sea but I can't help that."

I smile but can't help thinking of Freddie who would no doubt mirror my own choice and I wonder what he's doing now. I know he went to the local pub and I can't shake the bad feeling that accompanied me here when I think of him chatting up the barmaid with no strings attached. I, on the other hand, have ended up in a fairy story where all my dreams could be about to come true. I never thought for one moment that would ever happen when I agreed to come to Happy Ever After, but as Alex stares at me with those lust riddled eyes, I feel extremely hot indeed.

CHAPTER 28

By the time we finish up, I have learned that Alex lives alone in a house near Weymouth. His parents live nearby in one of the villages, and he has a brother and sister who have moved away from the area. He's not in a relationship and has only dated two girls seriously before. His ambition is to travel the world, preferably with a like-minded companion. His goal in life appears to be to get married, have two children and buy a house near the sea. As he speaks, my mind is telling me that he's perfect. He is everything I'm looking for and to reel him in before he gets away. My heart, however, just never showed up tonight and appears to have gone to the pub with the guys.

I listen politely and try to look interested, but something is holding me back. I have to ask myself, if I never met Freddie, would I think about this differently? I'm guessing I would because Alex ticks every box and even some in reserve.

When the waiter brings the bill, I make to pay and Alex closes his hand around mine and says softly, "My treat. I would never dream of asking you to pay."

As I stare into those gorgeous brown eyes, something shifts inside me. Maybe I'm not giving him the chance he deserves. Perhaps Saint Catherine saw something that I don't and Freddie is probably cosying up to the busty barmaid as we speak. I owe it to her to give this a chance, so when Alex takes my hand in his, I don't pull away and just smile at him shyly. Maybe I shouldn't encourage him because I'm not good at affairs of the heart but I am so desperate to meet someone and settle down, I'm willing to try anything and I'm guessing that being with Freddie, not that he's even asked, would not feel so safe, with doubt always on the horizon whenever an attractive woman catches his eye.

We make it back to the car and Alex helps me inside and now the night is in full swing and the stars are out in force. Before he starts the engine, he turns and says, "I'm not ready for the evening to end. Would you like to take a walk around the harbour?"

Cursing my bad judgement in wearing these heels, I try to act brave and smile. "That would be lovely."

We make the short drive around the harbour and find a convenient place to park, and once again Alex helps me out and takes my hand. Now the moon is out and the gentle lap of the waves creates an atmosphere of expectation and it feels so nice to promenade with a man like him.

We take a gentle walk around the harbour wall and I try so hard not to let the pain interfere with my romantic stroll and just bite my lip when the shoe rubs my toes and causes them to chafe.

"So, would you like to do this again, Susie? I hope I haven't scared you off."

"Yes, of course, it was, um, nice."

He stops and spins to face me and my heart starts thumping as he pulls me close and whispers, "Can I kiss you?"

I nod and as his lips touch mine, I wait for the fireworks to reinforce the legend. Surely this is love's true kiss and everything will slot into place. As kisses go, it's a nice one, soft, slightly hesitant and then firmer, more demanding. I test out my heart and am disappointed not to find fulfilment in there, but I suppose its early days. Alex appears happy though and runs his hand around the back of my head and holds it in place as he deepens the kiss. I must admit it's romantic, I mean, under the moon and stars with the waves lapping nearby is the stuff of every romance novel. Maybe it's my own doubts that are ruining this moment for me, and I should give Saint Catherine the benefit of the doubt and try a little harder.

When he pulls back, I am disappointed at the relief that follows it and curse my romantic heart for daring to expect better.

"That was amazing, Susie, I just knew we had a deep connection."

"Yes, it was."

He strokes my face lightly and stares deep into my eyes and smiles. "Meet me tomorrow and we can continue where we left off. Please say you will, I'm struggling to let you go at all."

"Well, if you insist."

I smile and he groans before crushing his lips to mine once again and I try a little harder this time. He is obviously sensing something that I'm missing and so I kiss him back, trying to get my head back into the romantic game.

"Get a room." Someone calls out as they drive past, and Alex pulls back and rests his head to mine and laughs softly. "I wouldn't mind, but I'm guessing that's a step too far. Instead, I'll drop you back with the promise of continuing where we left off tomorrow at the same time. Maybe I'll show you where I live and the places I go, let you discover a little more about me before you leave."

"That sounds great, I can't wait."

Once again, I smile brightly and try to join him in his happy place. What's wrong with me, something obviously is because if I had to choose a husband from a store specialising in them, surely I would choose a man like him, wouldn't I?

CHAPTER 29

Strangely, my first thought as soon as I wake up is of Freddie. He wasn't back when I returned last night, and I struggled to stay awake to wait for him. Now, in the cold light of day, I note with a sinking feeling that his side of the bed hasn't been slept in and I don't know why but I assume the worst – he stayed with *her*, the barmaid from the Frog and Lily.

The disappointment crushes me and I blink back tears as yet another delicious fantasy bites the dust. Then I feel angry at myself because I have no right to judge Freddie when I was out on a date with another man.

I don't even register the fact that it's a beautiful sunny day in Happy Ever After. It normally is, which is weird in itself. I suppose I'm so used to the grey skies of home, this is quite a novelty, but it may as well be raining for all I care because I feel so empty inside.

I shouldn't though. I should be waking with the joy of love in my heart if Saint Catherine has got it right. Alex couldn't have been more perfect except for one thing – he isn't Freddie.

Feeling as if I've lost something valuable, I take a moment to study the ring that still sparkles on my finger. I haven't taken it off since Alex gave it back to me in the most romantic of ways, except to switch fingers, but now it just mocks me. "It's all your fault." I whisper as I stare at it angrily. "Things were going along nicely before you fell on me. Now look what you've done, you've complicated my life and turned a relaxing break into a quest for love and happy endings. Shame on you."

Sighing, I drag myself from the cosy bed and stagger into the bathroom, my feet still sore from the torture they were inflicted last night by my ill-judged footwear choice.

The woman staring back at me in the mirror is a fool. A deluded fool who is looking for something where it obviously isn't. Maybe I should look at what's staring at me in the face and pursue my dream with Alex instead. He won't let me down and run off with the first woman who smiles at him with encouragement. Yes, Alex is my future and I need to step up and deal with it properly.

I head off to breakfast and see the fossil hunters are tucking in already, but still no sign of Freddie and my heart sinks. Where is he?

"Hi, Susie, did you have a nice evening?"

Thomas smiles as his friends all look at me with interest.

"Yes, lovely thanks, did you?"

Thomas nods. "We did thanks, it was fun."

Jacob looks a little worried, though. "Is Freddie ok this morning, we were a bit worried leaving him like that?"

What! I stare at him in surprise and shake my head. "I haven't seen him and I'm not sure if he came back at all."

George looks at Noah and they share a look I don't like in the slightest and Matty groans. "I told you we shouldn't leave him. I blame you for that Oliver, you were so keen to get back to watch Planet Earth, you didn't stop to think about Freddie."

"Why, what happened?" I almost dare not ask, and Oliver shrugs. "He looked to be enjoying himself and probably wouldn't have thanked us for the interruption. He was so deep in conversation with the barmaid all night, he may as well have been on his own, anyway."

His words are like steel blades against my heart and I feel like such a fool. Of course, he was with her. I suppose I knew all along he would be. Freddie Carlton just can't help himself and who am I to judge. He owes me nothing and is just in pursuit of his own happy ever after.

I smile brightly as they look at me with concern and we are interrupted as Eloise and Greg venture in, laughing between themselves. As soon as they see me, they stifle their grins and look a little guilty, which instantly makes me know something's up.

"Oh, hi, Susie, guys."

They take their seats and I take my own, looking miserably out of the window with half an ear on their conversation. Greg turns to the fossil table and laughs. "Next time you all go to the pub, let me tag along, Freddie looks as if he's had the night of his life."

I turn around as Eloise giggles. "Don't you dare, if you ever return in that state, I'll lock the door and you can spend the night on the porch."

"Why, what's happened to Freddie?"

Eloise looks at me with a hint of pity in her eyes. "We heard quite a commotion last night around midnight. Greg looked out because we were worried it was someone breaking into our car, it's on lease you know and we would be liable for any damage."

I feel so frustrated I want to scream, and she shakes her head. "You can never be too careful, you know. Anyway,

Greg told me he saw Freddie stumbling out of a car and the sound of a woman laughing."

They all look at me and I say tightly, "Don't look at me, I was sound asleep in bed."

I don't like the pity in their eyes as they try to cover it up and Eloise says in a calm voice, "Well, I'm sure it was nothing. Anyway, we watched him stagger down the path through the gardens and that's the last we saw of him. The girl was trying her best to hold him up, but they were laughing too much and kept on falling over. It was quite comical really."

Suddenly, the door opens and the man himself heads inside looking extremely worse for wear and I note how pale he looks and quite disturbed. He nods sheepishly and takes the seat opposite and rakes his fingers through his hair, looking a little traumatised if I'm honest. It strikes me that he won't even look me in the eye and just reaches for the water on the table and drains the glass.

"Good evening?"

My voice sounds tight and disapproving, and he nods. "Great, how about yours?"

"The best, actually. I had an amazing time. Alex was the perfect gentleman and so attentive and kind. I couldn't have wished for a better date, really."

"Oh."

I'm aware that all ears are on our conversation and stare at them pointedly, and they have the good sense to look away and carry on eating.

Sandra heads into the room and heads straight for us. "Good morning, what a lovely one it is. What can I make you to eat this morning? Full English with toast, or do you fancy eggs benedict or something else, an omelette perhaps?"

Freddie looks as if he may be sick at any moment and I say loudly, "Full English for me please, Sandra with toast and a side of pancakes, I'm feeling famished. Same for you, Freddie, as always?"

I smirk as he groans and shakes his head. "Just a coffee and a piece of toast please Sandra, I'm feeling a little fragile today."

To my surprise, Sandra looks at him with concern and lowers her voice. "I'm so sorry, Freddie, that was so unfortunate."

"It's fine." He looks at me quickly and I don't miss the slight shake of his head as he signals something to Sandra, but I'm not stupid. Something happened last night, and he doesn't want me to find out what it was.

Conversation is non-existent as Freddie broods on something and I feel so let down I can't even bear to look at him, let alone have a conversation. I still don't know why I'm so affected by him. We're not a couple, strangers really, but in my head, he was the man fate was supposed to deliver to me. Not Alex, Freddie, but now I understand why Saint Catherine intervened. I got it wrong as always, and I must just accept that and congratulate myself on a lucky escape.

To his credit, Freddie remains seated as I eat my way through one of Sandra's award winning breakfasts. It must be agony because he looks as if he may be sick at any moment and I hope he's suffering.

As soon as I finish, I push my plate away and sigh with contentment. "That was amazing. I'm sorry you're not feeling up to one yourself, do you think you've caught a bug, or was it too much to drink last night?"

Freddie shrugs and makes to say something but obviously thinks better of it and the silence falls between us. Remembering what we are supposed to be doing today, I say quickly, "Are we still going on that appointment, or are you going to cancel due to ill health?"

"No, we're going." Freddie sighs and I say brightly, "Did you ask Lizzie, is she waiting for us outside?"

I don't miss the blind panic on Freddie's face as he shakes his head vigorously and lowers his voice. "No, she doesn't know, and please don't tell her. Let's just try to slip out unnoticed and leave - preferably forever."

I stare at him in confusion and then to my surprise, he stands, grabs my hand and almost pulls my arm out of its socket as he races quickly out of the room.

CHAPTER 30

I almost can't catch my breath as he pulls me towards his car with a sense of urgency and manage to squeak, "Stop!"

He shakes his head. "I'm sorry, Susie, I think we should just place a little distance between me and Happy Ever After today."

He unlocks his car and I say firmly, "We'll take my car, I don't want you driving in your state and you could be arrested for driving under the influence."

"By your boyfriend I suppose." Freddie's voice is laced with sarcasm and I say quickly, "No, thanks to your girlfriend plying you with drinks all night, she should be reported for encouraging alcoholism."

"Kimberly didn't encourage anything; she was really kind as it happens."

"You would say that."

"Meaning?"

I open my mouth to deliver a crushing retort but Freddie turns pale and says quickly, "Your car it is, hurry."

I shrug and rummage in my bag for the keys and Freddie

looks around with a worried expression, making me wonder what really did happen last night and as we squash our bodies into the car, he hisses, "Just drive, please."

As we head off up the driveway, I look in my rear-view mirror and see Lizzie and the Major walking arm in arm and wonder what they've got to do with Freddie's obvious reluctance to meet up with anyone and why was Sandra apologising?

Suddenly, I start to giggle and Freddie says tightly, "What's so funny?"

"You're scared of Lizzie and the Major, something happened last night, it's obvious. Come on, Freddie, you can tell me."

"Stop, nothing happened."

"So, it did, this is priceless. Tell me."

"Nothing happened." Freddie's voice is tight, and he looks out of the window and I can't stop giggling. After a while, he says irritably, "Anyway, don't you even want to know where we're going, we can't just drive with nowhere to go."

"Ok, tell me."

"What, the directions, or what happened last night?"

"Both."

He groans and says in a pained voice, "Ok, I'll programme your Sat Nav and then I'll tell you what was probably the most traumatic event in my life, while you were enjoying your cosy one to one with Prince Charming."

Now I'm so curious I almost don't want to wait for him to enter the address, but after an agonising few minutes, he accomplishes it after cursing several times when he enters the wrong postcode and has to re-enter the information.

Then he says with a sigh, "I had a great time with the guys. They were fun to be around, but when they started talking about fossils and stuff, I sort of tuned out a little. It's not really my thing, so I started chatting to Kimberly, you know, the barmaid we met on our first day."

"I know who Kimberly is." I say tightly and Freddie nods. "Yes, a great girl, so friendly and keen to chat."

"I bet she was." I can't stop myself because just the mention of her makes jealousy rear its ugly head, even though it has no reason doing so.

"Anyway, we chatted most of the night and I suppose I had a little too much to drink. The guys were leaving, and I was having a good time, so Kimberly told them she'd drop me back when her shift finished."

My hands grip the wheel tightly as I picture the two of them enjoying a cosy evening 'chatting' and I swallow the harsh retort I want to hit him with because I have absolutely no right to pass comment.

"Anyway, I don't know what they put in their drinks but it's powerful stuff and as soon as the air hit me, I was gone."

"That would be the rohypnol."

"The what?"

"Rohypnol she probably put in your drink."

"Don't be ridiculous, of course Kimberly didn't drug me, why would she?"

"Because she fancies you, Freddie, it's obvious."

"Not to me it isn't, anyway, what do you know, you weren't there. You were enjoying loves' young dream with a figment of women's fantasies everywhere."

I fall silent because this conversation is doing neither of us any favours and Freddie sighs. "Anyway, do you want to know what happened without constantly interrupting me?"

"Of course, sorry go on."

"Anyway," he sighs "she said she'd help me find my room because for some reason, I couldn't walk particularly well and we bumped into Kevin on the way. It turns out he knows Kimberly, and they had a nice chat while I stood there swaying. Kevin must have noticed I wasn't myself and offered to make me a coffee in his man cave. Apparently, it's behind the house and it's where he goes to escape it all. In his case, it's an escape *from* Happy Ever After."

He laughs and I shake my head. "Then what happened?"

"Well, we both went with him and it's quite surprising in there. I mean, he has a log burner and everything and it's a really cosy cabin. Apparently, he works there, it's his office and there were filing cabinets and a desk and everything an office needs. Anyway, we sat on his settee next to the log burner and Kevin made us a coffee. It was the least we could do to thank Kimberly for her kindness, and everything was going well. I'm not sure what they were talking about because there was a strange buzzing in my head, but after a while that stopped."

"So, what were they talking about?"

"Oh, you know local stuff. Anyway, the coffee did the trick and I suppose we got a little carried away and stayed there for a bit."

"A bit."

My heart sinks picturing Freddie and Kimberly curled up on the cosy settee in front of a flickering fire, and Freddie nods. "I'm not sure what time it was and the next thing I knew it was morning and when I woke up, I couldn't remember much of what happened the night before. I was still in the cabin but…"

He breaks off and the alarm bells start ringing loud and clear. "But what?"

He whispers, "I wasn't alone."

Immediately, I picture the worst and imagine a naked Kimberly curled around him after a night of passion and Freddie says in a very troubled voice, "I'm not sure I can deal with what happened, and it's all your fault for leaving me."

"My fault, are you serious?"

He sighs heavily. "Of course, it was your fault, you went off with another man and left me exposed to predators."

"Kimberly."

The silence gives me my answer and then Freddie says in a very disturbed voice, "Lizzie."

I almost crash the car as I yell, "What the…Lizzie, oh my god, you didn't…"

"I don't know."

"Freddie!"

I pull over to the side of the road and look at him in shock and he looks so traumatised, I reach for his hand. "I'm so sorry, do you know if you… um?"

"No. It's awful, Susie, I woke up naked and wrapped in a blanket on the settee. Lizzie was sleeping beside me in a nightie and then Sandra came in."

I am trying hard not to laugh at the picture he is painting and try instead to look like a counsellor or something with a professional detachment, but really, this is hilarious, poor Freddie.

"The thing is, Susie, when Sandra yelled her name, Lizzie just opened one eye and grinned. It was horrible. I felt as if I had been violated and couldn't remember a thing."

"Probably the rohypnol."

"Will you stop saying that, Kimberly did not drug my drink, I told you she was so kind. Anyway, Sandra asked her mother outright if she had interfered with me. Yes, she actually said that word and I was so mortified I couldn't speak. Lizzie just laughed and said a lady never tells and actually winked at me. I'm sorry, Susie, but what if…"

"It's ok, Freddie, I'm sure nothing happened. Lizzie probably just found you sleeping and well…"

"Exactly, it doesn't look good, does it?"

He looks so upset, I instinctively reach for him and pull him close and his arms wrap around me and it feels nice. I'm not sure why, but Freddie's arms around me feel right, as if they are familiar and not awkward like it was last night with Alex. I can feel our hearts thumping and something shifts in the atmosphere. Almost at the same time, we pull back and stare into each other's eyes and I see the longing in his that catches me off guard. His mouth is centimetres from mine and I feel a flutter in my heart that has never been there before. Suddenly, all I want in life is to share a kiss with this man and I lean forward a little and my breath hitches and I close my eyes.

Then the moment is gone as his phone rings and cursing, he pulls away and answers with a curt, "Yes!"

There's a short silence, and he says apologetically, "Oh, I'm sorry, hi Monica, yes, um, the Sat Nav says ten minutes. …yes, ok, see you soon."

He looks at me with an expression of regret and resignation and says in a low voice, "She's waiting. We had better leave."

"Of course." I clear my throat and gather my senses around me as I start the engine and am left with yet another question needing an answer. If we had just kissed, would that have changed everything?

CHAPTER 31

*A*s soon as we stop outside the dilapidated ruin that Freddie is considering buying, I fall in love. The large shell of a house that is held up by ivy, tears at my heartstrings as I picture what it once was. It is set in its own grounds that look as if the wicked fairy in Sleeping Beauty created the enchanted forest around it and I even see the remnants of a grand sweeping driveway that is now home to weeds and ruin.

Freddie steps forward to greet the estate agent and for a moment I am left to admire the view. This place is magical. It may be in urgent need of repair but it is breath-taking. Looking around, I can see nothing but nature. The air is still and the only sound is from the birds overhead and I am mesmerised.

As houses go, it's a project that could take a lifetime but I can see past that and imagine its magnificence if it was lucky to find someone who loved it enough to try.

Freddie heads back and stands beside me and says in a low whisper, "What do you think?"

"I think…" For some reason, I reach for his hand and squeeze it, before saying, "It's perfect."

He turns to look at me and for some reason raises my hand and the ring sparkles against the sun. He looks at the diamond and then into my eyes and I make to speak but the estate agent calls out, "It's unlocked, you can go inside."

He drops my hand and his expression makes me giggle as he whispers, "I'm not sure if I can, what if…"

"We'll go in together. Come on, Freddie, if there are spiders there, we won't look, just concentrate on the vision in your head of what you could make of this place."

He nods and swallows hard and to my surprise, laces his fingers with mine. "For protection."

He winks and I smile shyly as I follow him to the huge oak front door, trying not to look in the corners for unwelcome predators.

The inside of the house is as bad as the outside. The staircase looks rickety but I picture it when it was new and standing majestically in the entrance as a statement of splendour. The hallway itself is a big room and I can only imagine the parties the inhabitants must have enjoyed when it was filled with laughter and life. For some reason, the memories are ringing in my ears as I step into the past. It's as if I've come home because this house feels familiar, it's a happy place and has an air of mystery surrounding it that makes me wish Lolita Sharples was here right now to tell us what went on here in the past.

I am so caught up in the moment, it takes me a while to register that Monica is giving us a potted history of the house and I listen with interest as she speaks.

"The house was owned by a Thomas Jefferson, a local wealthy banker who worked in London but kept the house as a country home. His family owned it and I believe it belonged to their family and it passed to him when they died.

He was responsible for extensive refurbishment in the 1950s and by all accounts, it was ahead of its time."

"What happened then?" Freddie is interested and so am I, as Monica says sadly, "He died unexpectedly and didn't have an heir. The house and his affairs were held in trust while an heir was located but all they could find was a distant cousin in New Zealand. They inherited the house, land and his flat in London but never came to claim them. Instead, they left them to deteriorate and it's only when the heir died and it all passed to his son that things started to happen. The flat in London was always rented out but that was sold and now it's Lake View House's turn. The owner has no need for it and just wants to sell the land and have the money, which is why it's such a good price."

Freddie looks around thoughtfully. "How easy do you think it would be to get planning permission to restore it, or even knock it down and start again?"

I stare at him in horror. "Knock it down, are you serious? This place is amazing, you can't destroy something so beautiful."

He raises his eyes. "You think this is beautiful?"

"I do." I look around and a feeling of such overwhelming sadness grips me as I picture what this house could have been. "This house may be ruined but it's heart's still beating. Just think how amazing it could be if you restored it."

Monica nods her approval. "You know, it's always been a fascinating house for the locals. Most people don't know it's here because of the woods surrounding it but the lake, well, that's a place everybody should see once in their lives."

"The lake?" Freddie looks interested and Monica smiles. "I'll show you the grounds once you've finished looking around. I would advise against going upstairs because the staircase is on its last legs and may be dangerous. I can tell you that it has eight bedrooms and two bathrooms as well as a huge loft that could provide more accommodation when renovated. Downstairs are five reception rooms and a small kitchen that could be made larger by knocking a few rooms into one. There's a scullery and a boot room and a rather impressive drawing room looking out across what was once a landscaped garden. The house could be amazing but will take a lot of money to achieve, which is why it's going for such a good price."

She looks at Freddie with a hopeful expression and my heart sinks. This is a major project and a certain money pit. I'm guessing Freddie doesn't have the money to take on a project of this magnitude and I say a little sadly, "Maybe you should think about this, Freddie. I'm not sure if it's worth your investment. It could drain every bit of money you have and become a burden. No matter how amazing it could be, you would have a difficult time achieving that and maybe you should have a good long hard think about it first."

Monica throws me daggers as I scupper her sales pitch and Freddie nods. "You're right, Susie, I must think long and hard and will certainly not make a decision today."

He looks at Monica and smiles. "I'd like to see the grounds now."

She nods and we follow her outside, just as the sun shows itself through the trees and lights up the landscape.

I gasp as I see the sparkle of water through a gap in the trees and Freddie says in disbelief, "Wow."

Monica nods, "It's the most impressive part of this property, go and discover why."

Freddie grasps my hand tightly and we race off at a brisk pace through the trees towards the sparkling water and as we step outside into a clearing, what lies before us takes my breath away.

CHAPTER 32

Like the rarest jewel, a huge lake dominates the area that lies surrounded by lush greenery and trees. The only life it seems are the ducks enjoying the sunshine and paddling around their amazing home. The lake is so big a stone bridge separates it and taking Freddie's hand; I race towards it like a child, squealing in pleasure. "Wow, Freddie, this is like a fairy tale. I love it."

He laughs as he runs to keep up and says teasingly, "I thought you didn't run."

"Only in exceptional cases and what's better than this. Just look, there's a waterfall on the other side of the bridge, that ends up in a stream along the grassy bank. I never knew such amazing places existed; the estate agent was right. The lake *is* the jewel in the crown.

As I stare around, I can't believe my eyes. Weeping willows and grassy banks are set beside the tranquil lake, and I imagine picnics with wicker baskets and floral blankets as the children play their games nearby while the parents enjoy the sunshine. I imagine those children fishing with nets and playing chase and paddling in the lake on a hot and balmy day. The simple pleasures of life are right here, and I can't believe this place has remained empty so long.

We begin our walk around the lake and Freddie says thoughtfully, "You know, it is a big investment and could take several years."

"Not to mention lots of money, more than I would probably make in a lifetime."

"It is pretty fantastic though."

I nod and stand beside him and look back in the direction of the house that is screened behind the trees, standing like proud soldiers guarding their castle.

"Would you really move down here, or is it just an investment you're looking for?"

He pulls me down beside him on the grassy bank and to my surprise, rests his arm around my shoulder. It feels so nice I lean into him and he rubs my arm with a distraction that betrays how much he's thinking about this.

"The thing is, I need to shake my life up a bit. The barn I converted in Surrey is worth a lot more than I paid for it, despite all the money I spent. My business is going well and I could work anywhere really, but this, it may be a step too far and kind of lonely if I moved here."

"I'm guessing you wouldn't be lonely for long." I can't help the bitterness in my voice as I picture the barmaid and he shrugs. "Maybe not, but we both know I can't be trusted to make the right decision when it concerns women. Anyway, what about you, things are shaping up nicely that may mean you have a decision of your own to make? I wonder if PC Perfect would be happy to move to your flat in Slipend."

"Are you jealous of Alex, Freddie?"

I giggle because he sounds as annoyed at the mention of Alex as I am Kimberly and he shrugs. "It's nothing to do with me, it's your life and you must trust your own judgement. He seems ok I suppose but just be careful and don't make any rash decisions. I have a feeling we're both capable of that, which is why I'm going to think about buying Lake View house when I get home to normality. Here it's tempting to throw caution to the wind and jump in feet first, but I don't want to find my boots leak and regret my decision."

We sit for a moment, both of us with a different problem to solve, and then Freddie takes my hand and rubs his finger over the ring that sparkles in the sunshine. "Do you regret finding this ring, Susie?"

"Why do you ask?"

"I don't know." He shrugs. "It just complicates your life a little. I suppose you have to ask yourself if you would be trying with the policeman if you hadn't found the ring. If he's everything you were looking for and you would be interested under normal circumstances, I would be happy for you, but I'm worried you're blinded by romance and the opinions of quite frankly dubious locals. Maybe you should head home before making any rash decisions."

I look at the ring and smile. "I'm not sure that regret is the right word. I'm ecstatic I found the ring and interested in the story surrounding it. The locals have given me an insight into the myth but I'm a great believer in fate and something is telling me I was always meant to find mine here, in Happy Ever After. You know, I almost didn't come, but I woke up one day with the realisation I must, something important was going to happen to me here and now I know what it was - the ring."

He nods and smiles but he doesn't look happy for me and he makes to speak but then his phone rings again and he sighs. "Hi, sorry, we're just coming."

"Monica?"

He nods. "Apparently she has another viewing at 12.30 and needs to go. She said we could come back tomorrow, but I think I've seen enough, have you?"

I look around at the perfect paradise and think that I will never get enough of this view, but I smile and make to stand. "Yes, come on, I'll treat you to a cream tea on the way home. We haven't had one yet and I believe that's the law in Dorset and god forbid I get arrested for neglecting to sample Dorset's finest scones."

We head back and after Freddie exchanges a few words with Monica, we turn our back on Lake View house and I feel it tearing at my heartstrings. There is something special about this house, I just know it.

CHAPTER 33

Freddie and I enjoy a scrumptious cream tea in a cosy tea room in the nearby village. Like me, he heaps the jam on first, followed by the cream and orders a breakfast tea rather than a filter coffee. I am getting used to us liking the same things and Freddie is easy company and the conversation never dries up. Over the scones and clotted cream, he tells me about his family and the pranks they always play and I laugh and share a few of my own stories from work that make him almost choke a few times.

As soon as we leave and get in the car, he says flippantly, "So, what are your plans this evening? Have you got another date with destiny, or do you fancy heading into the nearest town for a look?"

I feel bad and say apologetically, "Actually, I'm having dinner with Alex, he kind of insisted."

"I see."

He doesn't say anything else and I feel so bad I blurt out, "You could come with us if you like."

He laughs out loud. "You are joking. No, I doubt your new friend would be happy about that, No, I'll find Kimberly and see if she fancies keeping me company, it's fine, have a nice time."

Why do I feel so desperate whenever he mentions her, and why do I wish I wasn't seeing Alex and could spend the evening with him? It's obvious now why I'm still single because even a fairy tale come true can't point me in the right direction, which I'm convinced is Alex. All the facts add up and point to him except for one very important one, I'm not as attracted to him half as much as I am to Freddie and I enjoy Freddie's company more. Then again, Freddie has so many options, I'm sure the barmaid is just a drop in the ocean.

Our journey back to Happy Ever After is a quiet one as we both fall silent and the easy camaraderie we shared before is slipping away as circumstances pull us in different directions.

∽

THE FIRST PERSON we see when we stop in the parking bay is Lizzie and Freddie groans. "Do you think she's seen us?"

"I'd say that's a definite because she's waving at you and is heading over."

"Please protect me, Susie, that woman scares the hell out of me."

Lizzie raps on the window and I lower it, using my master control switch and laugh to myself as Freddie sinks lower in his seat.

"Hey, handsome, you ran off before we got a chance to catch up this morning. I think we need to talk."

Freddie looks at me helplessly as Lizzie giggles and winks at me. "He's a hot one, that's for sure. I'm sorry, Susie, I couldn't help myself."

Freddie is staring at her in horror and she smiles and flutters her eyelashes. "Come with me, Kevin's been looking for you, he has something you may want to hear."

Freddie looks at me helplessly and I smile. "Go on, I just need to make a call of nature, I'll meet you in the room."

He heads off with Lizzie hanging off his arm and I laugh to myself at the dejected look on his face as they disappear from view.

I take the time to relax a little in a room that is more than fit for the job. Everything about Happy Ever After is perfect. The room, the setting and the people, although they are a little strange, make this a very pleasant stay indeed and I wonder how I'll feel when I pack my many bags and head home to Slipend.

Reaching for my book, I take a few moments to settle back against the pillows on the huge bed and read a few pages, but for some reason, I can't concentrate. There is so much swirling around my head it's impossible to put anything else there, so with a sigh, I shut the book and lean back and stare at the ceiling. I should feel happy. I should feel excited and I should feel *something* for Alex because there is absolutely nothing wrong with him. It's just me, I'm not interested and maybe I should just accept that I'm not the rightful owner of the ring. Saint Catherine delivered me someone else's fairy tale because if it was meant to be Alex, I would be wildly in love right now - surely.

I must drift off to sleep because when I wake, it's getting dark and my stomach growls, reminding me to feed it. Looking at the clock by my bed, I notice it's nearly 7pm and jump up in a panic. Rubbing my eyes, I look around me in disbelief; where's Freddie and why didn't he wake me?

Quickly, I scramble to my feet and head inside the bathroom to restore some form of normality to my face and cursing, I stumble around the room, desperately trying to get ready for my impending date with destiny. I don't have time to take the same trouble over my appearance and just brush my hair, throw on some lip gloss and change into some smart leggings and a floaty top. Grabbing my smart jacket, I slip on some pumps – no high heels for me tonight, I learned that lesson at least and I grab my bag and head out to meet him.

As I walk, I wonder where Freddie is. Did he come back and think better of disturbing me, or is he still with Lizzie? I laugh to myself as I picture them together and the devastation on his face. I'm pretty sure nothing did happen last night, but it's funny watching him squirm about it.

As I turn the corner, I see Alex waiting, looking handsome as he leans against his car, and as I walk towards him, I give myself a stern talking to. Look at him, he is more than good enough. Any woman, man or beast would be glad to attract his interest and I need to try hard tonight to see if there's something there at least.

He smiles as I approach and then, to my horror, I trip and fall straight into his outstretched arms. Laughing, he holds me up and his arms wrap around me, keeping me safe.

"Oops, sorry." I laugh and make to pull away but instead he pulls me closer and whispers huskily, "We can't waste this opportunity, I missed you today."

I look up into his dark eyes that glitter with interest and prepare myself for the kiss that I know is coming. As his lips find mine, I wait for the fireworks, but not tonight because as we connect, I feel nothing. There is no passion and I am just going through the motions and above everything, I just want it to end in case anyone sees us.

What is wrong with me?

Alex pulls back and strokes my cheek, whispering, "I can't believe I found you. I'm a lucky man."

I make to speak because I feel so bad, but he places his

finger on my lips and whispers, "You don't have to say it, I know."

He knows – what? That I'm just not feeling it, or does he think I feel the same? I don't even get a chance to ask, before he says briskly, "Come on, let me show you some of the sights."

He helps me into his car like the gentleman he is, and as the door closes, my heart sinks. What am I doing here?

CHAPTER 34

Alex takes me on a tour of the area and even in the darkness, I can tell it's an amazing place. He shows me where he works, went to school and as we pull up outside a smart little row of houses, he says proudly, "This is my home. Would you like to take a look around?"

"Yes, of course."

My heart beats a little faster as I follow him inside the smart terraced house, and as the door closes, I wonder if I'm doing the right thing here. Perhaps we should have gone somewhere more public. I'm not usually one to place myself in an awkward situation, but then again, he is a police officer. Surely, I'm safe with him.

Alex is proud of his home, it's obvious as he shows me around a very neat and tidy space. His taste is modern and clutter free and there isn't a cushion out of place it is that tidy. There are no pictures, no books, no magazines, no objects at all to tell me who this man is, and it's a far cry from my own cluttered paradise in the flat I share.

We end up in the kitchen and he reaches for the kettle. Would you like a coffee, or maybe something stronger?

"Oh, a coffee would be nice, thank you."

As he busies himself preparing it, he says lightly, "I could phone for a food delivery and we could stay in and watch a film, or there's a great show on Netflix you may want to see."

My stomach growls reminding me it's empty and I smile brightly, "Sounds good what do you fancy?" He raises his eyes and throws me a lust filled look and I say hastily, "To eat, um, I quite like pizza."

"Then pizza it is, I'll give them a call."

As soon as he makes the coffee, he grabs his phone and rattles off an order and then hangs up and grins. "Come on, let's make ourselves comfortable in the living room. I'll put the film on and we can wait for the food."

Nervously, I follow him in and sit perched on the edge of the settee as he fiddles with the remote. Then he leans back, dragging me with him and says huskily, "This is nice, isn't it?"

I just nod and try to look interested in the film, but I'm panicking inside. This feels so wrong, I'm not sure why, it just does.

Luckily, watching a film means we don't have to make conversation and I soon relax a little and just enjoy the show. Around thirty minutes later, the doorbell rings and the pizza arrives, which also kills some time and as we devour the treat from heaven, or in this case, the local Dominos, I begin to relax a little. Alex is trying hard and I should lower my guard a little and give him the benefit of the doubt.

After a while, he says with interest, "How much longer before you head home?"

"Just two days, can you believe it, it's all gone so quickly."

He shakes his head and sighs. "Don't go."

"Pardon me."

"Stay here. You can stay with me for a while, look for a job locally, I don't know, take an extended holiday, just please don't leave."

"But…" He shakes his head. "The thing is, Susie, now that I've found you, I want to see where this is going. We can't do that from a distance and I can't just leave my job. Please stay at least for a couple of weeks. We owe it to Saint Catherine to give this our best shot." He smiles and then laughs softly. "Please forgive me, I'm not usually this full on, but well, I've never been in this situation before. If you leave in a couple of days, I'm worried we won't give this – us, the chance it deserves. Will you at least consider it?"

I stare at him in confusion and his face softens, and he leans closer, taking my hand in his and lifting the one bearing the ring. "This is a sign that we were meant to be together. I'm a great believer in destiny, Susie, and this is ours. Stay here with me and fall in love. What can be more important than that?"

He leans in and presses his lips to mine and this time there's no holding back – on his part, anyway. He deepens the kiss and pulls me closer, and I feel as if I'm drowning. It's all too much, I'm not being given time to think. He's crowding me and making me face something I'm not ready to. He groans and pulls me closer and his hands start to wander and I panic inside. I'm not ready to move this thing on, I don't want to, but why not? He's perfect, he's the one. I know he is.

I squeeze my eyes tightly shut and try to get in the zone. I must try harder. Fate is delivering me my happy ever after and I need to accept her gift with gratitude. I kiss him back and look for those flutters that tell me I want him. Surely, they are there. But all I feel is blind panic and trapped in a situation that is now getting out of control. As Alex pushes me back on the settee, I push him away and say quickly, "Alex, please, I need to think about this."

He looks disappointed and I feel bad, but then he nods

and smiles. "Of course, I'm sorry Susie, it's just that, well, I can't keep my hands off you."

"No." I smile weakly. "I'm sorry, I'm not sure what's the matter with me lately, but I suppose a lot has happened and I'm still playing catch up. If it's ok with you, can we wait a bit? I would like some time to adjust and everything's happening so fast, I'm struggling to keep up."

He takes my hand and squeezes it, looking so genuine I feel bad and want nothing more than to cry. "Take as long as you like, darling. I admit it's happening fast, but it *is* happening, can't you feel it?"

The trouble is, that's the problem, I don't – feel it. I look down at the ring that sits on my finger like a ball and chain, and say in a whisper, "Fate works in mysterious ways, maybe it was fate that brought me this ring, or maybe I was just in the right place at the right time, it's a big responsibility that came with it though."

He takes my hand and laces his fingers with mine and whispers, "It is, but it also brings great excitement. I'm sorry I'm rushing things and ordinarily I wouldn't but we don't have the luxury of time. I suppose, I'm so desperate to convince you to stay, I'm coming on a little strong. What do you say to heading to the pub and lightening the atmosphere a little? Think about my offer and give it some serious consideration. If you decide to return home, we can make it work. I'll come to Slipend on my days off and you can spend some time here. We owe it to ourselves to try at least."

I smile weakly and he says firmly, "Come on, I'll take you to a sweet little pub I think you'll like, and we'll think about ways to make this work. No pressure though." He smiles, and I feel relieved. No pressure sounds really good right now and as I follow him out, I am hopeful that fate will intervene and show me the way because left to my own devices, I'm sure to make every mistake in the book.

CHAPTER 35

Despite my reservations, I do enjoy Alex's company. Who wouldn't? He's good looking, charming, funny and eager to please. There's just no spark, no insane attraction that I need in a relationship, and I'm starting to doubt the power of the ring. By the time he drops me back to Happy Ever After, I think I've made up my mind. Despite the legend, the ring, the whole romantic scenario, I am not going to take this any further.

However, as soon as we pull up, I see Freddie in the distance with his arm slung around Kimberly and it's like a physical pain to my heart. It thumps so hard when I see her reach up and wipe some kind of imaginary speck off his face, and he laughs before dipping his face to whisper something in her ear that makes her laugh.

"Is that your friend?"

Alex's voice cuts through my pain and I nod miserably. "Yes, Freddie is the guy I'm sharing with."

"It looks as if he's found his happy ever after too. What can I say, this place is legendary?"

He laughs and I try to find the humour in the situation

but can't and just shrug. "Yes, well, if you ask me, he didn't have to try too hard. They met on the first night and have been inseparable ever since."

I watch as they look up as the car comes to a stop and my heart sinks when I see they are heading our way. Feeling the devil control my senses, I smile at Alex. "Thank you so much for a great evening, I really enjoyed myself."

"Me too Susie, I always do when I'm with you."

His eyes glitter and he leans towards me but just before his lips touch mine, somebody knocks on the window and we pull back quickly.

"Suze, come and meet Kimberly, she's dying to see you again."

Trying hard to control my hatred of the woman, I plaster a smile on my face and open the door as Alex does the same.

He heads my way and stands beside me and looks at Freddie with undisguised curiosity, and it strikes me that Freddie is not that happy to see him.

Kimberly, to her credit, beams at us both and says happily, "Susie, we never really got the chance to meet properly. Freddie has told me so much about you and what happened at Saint Catherine's Chapel. I can't believe it; you must be so excited."

She glances down at the ring and squeals. "Is that it, can I take a look? I can't believe I'm really seeing it."

Holding up my hand, I have to admit the ring is beautiful and Kimberly grabs my hand and says enviously, "You are sooo lucky, isn't she Freddie. You know, I'm betting the local radio station would be so interested in this love story." She looks at Alex and says with excitement, "The police officer and the tourist, joined together by a legend. We should call them." She turns to Freddie and squeals. "Can we? It's such a romantic story, please I know someone who works on the reception. She would make sure it reached the right person and…"

"No!"

We turn and look at Alex in surprise as he shakes his head. "I'm sorry, no publicity, it wouldn't be a good idea because I'm a police officer and I don't want people knowing that."

"Why not?" Freddie interrupts and Alex shakes his head.

"Listen, it's not an easy job and if people knew, they would make life difficult for me. It's not fair on Susie either, because the last thing she needs is people delving into her life and judging her."

"Why would they do that, she's done nothing to be ashamed of?" Freddie's tone is curt and I look at Alex in surprise, "I wouldn't mind, I haven't done anything wrong."

Alex exhales sharply and pulls me close and whispers, "I'm sorry, Susie, but not everyone is as broad-minded as we are. I would hate for you to be dragged through something you don't deserve. No, it's best if we keep this just between friends, for the moment at least."

Kimberly interrupts. "It may be too late for that."

"What do you mean?" Alex looks at her with a look that can only be described as blind panic, and Kimberly smirks. "A reporter for the Daily Telegraph is also a guest here, and we were just talking with him. He would love to do a write up on it and if he does, the local news will definitely be in touch. If you ask me, it's your duty because it was found in a national monument. Maybe you should get your story in first in case people think it's shady."

"Shady, are you serious?" Alex looks so angry I feel a little worried and Freddie nods. "It can't hurt, surely. I mean, one mention in the local news and then everyone will forget about it."

I think I've got a headache coming on and Alex says in a

calm voice. "Listen, we'll think about it. Susie has a lot to deal with at the moment and doesn't really have time for all this. She came here for a holiday and the last thing she needs is the attention this will bring."

"Why?" Freddie's tone is hard and Alex looks at him with a flash of annoyance.

"Listen, not everyone is as broad-minded as we are and wouldn't understand her choice of profession. I don't want her morals questioned when the public learns what she does for a living. It wouldn't be fair and if any of you care for her, you won't drag her though a humiliating process."

I stare at him in shock as Freddie hisses, "Her profession is nothing to be embarrassed about and Susie is the most moral person I know. How dare you suggest otherwise."

I watch Kimberly place her hand on Freddie in warning, as Alex tenses up and I say quickly, "Anyway, Alex is right. Maybe it's best for no publicity for the time being. We need to think about this. Well, I'm tired and need my beauty sleep. We should all calm down and get some sleep."

Inside I feel so hurt by Alex's words and need some time to digest them and I am feeling so emotional right now, I can't be trusted with any important decisions and just want this evening to end.

Alex turns to me and smiles. "Anyway, I should be heading off, but I have a day off tomorrow and wondered if you would like to spend the day together. We could grab a picnic and head to Durdle Door. You would love it there."

I watch Kimberly share a look with Freddie, and I push aside the hurt and smile. "Sounds good, what time?"

"Say 10ish. I'll pick you up then."

It feels a little awkward saying goodbye to Alex in front of spectators and so I nod and step back a little.

"Ok, great, um, I'll see you tomorrow. I'll look forward to it."

He hesitates a minute and then nods to the others and steps back into his car. We watch him leave and I hear Kimberly say brightly, "I must be going too. It was lovely to meet you, Susie, maybe we'll see each other again tomorrow, you never know." She smiles and head across to her own car and I'm just grateful they didn't say their goodbyes in front of me.

We watch her car disappear from view and Freddie surprises me by saying, "Come with me, Susie, there's something you should know."

CHAPTER 36

Rather than head towards our room, he guides me down the cobbled pathway towards the back of the house. "Where are we going, what's happening, it's so late, can't this wait?" My words come out in a jumble and Freddie says in a hard voice, "No, it can't."

I'm mystified as he walks beside me, and I can almost taste the tension in the air. What's happening?

I can smell the wood smoke in the air coming from the chimney protruding from the wooden cabin nestling in the clearing at the back of the house, and I say with concern. "Is this regarding the incident with Lizzie, has something happened?"

"What?"

I can just make out his puzzled look in the light of the moon and I laugh softly. "So, it wasn't what you thought."

"No – thank God." He laughs softly. "Apparently, she came in to do some digging, although I'm not sure what she meant by that and noticed me passed out on the couch. Well, to cut a long story short, she took her chance and made me more comfortable, as she put it and removed my bulky clothing. Then she decided to keep me company in case I needed help in the night. She apologised and told me not to think badly of her because a woman of her age needs to seize every opportunity she gets to make a memory worth remembering."

"Are you kidding me?"

I stare at him in shock and he laughs out loud. "Gross, isn't it? I mean, let this be the last time we ever speak of it. I don't think I want to take that memory with me into old age."

I start to laugh and he nudges me and I almost fall over. "Anyway, what about you and your Prince Charming, what's the situation there?"

At the mention of Alex, I stiffen up and wonder what I should tell him. It's obvious he's interested in Kimberly and if I tell him I'm having second thoughts about the whole legend thing, it will leave me looking more of a loser in love than I already am, so I paste a smile on my face and say airily, "It's going well. I mean, you heard him arrange to meet me tomorrow. Things are going great. Anyway, what about you and Kimberly, isn't it?"

"Me." He looks surprised. "Kimberly's just a friend. I told you. She's good company, I like her but not in that way. I thought you knew that?"

"No, I didn't."

I stare at him in horror as I think about the hours I've wasted picturing them together and then he reaches out and grasps my arm, making me stop in my tracks and pulls me around to face him.

"You really thought…"

"I did."

The only light is that of the moon as he stares into my eyes and whispers, "I thought you knew."

"That you liked her, I thought you did."

"Not *her*, Susie, not in that way. It was… anyway, it doesn't matter now, we need to get going."

He makes to leave and I pull him back and say slightly breathlessly, "Knew what, Freddie?"

I think the whole of my future balances on this moment as he rakes his fingers through his hair again, which he always seems to do when he's nervous, and then shifts a little closer and takes my hand.

"The only person that interests me, although God only knows why, is you, Susie Mahoney. Since the moment you barged into my hotel room and ordered me to leave, I knew I was interested. When you speak, I know what you're going to say before the sentence finishes. When you look at me, I see a woman I could easily spend the rest of my life with and when you're not with me, I feel an empty space beside me that makes me physically ache. You are a bad decision, a promise of trouble for my heart and someone who is bound to make my life hell, but I can't get enough of you. The trouble is, we both know I'm a man of bad decisions and poor judgement, which is why I chose a woman who was destined for another. Life sucks sometimes."

He looks so vulnerable standing there after having laid his heart on the line, it brings tears to my eyes.

He smiles ruefully and turns to leave and I say quickly, "Wait."

As he turns, I swallow the lump in my throat and say in a whisper, "You're interested in…me?"

He nods. "You make it impossible not to be. Don't worry though, I know my timing is off and you have this big romance going on but well, if anything goes wrong, put me down as a back-up. These shoulders are broad and they can take a lot of crying on."

"But…"

"It's ok, you don't need to say anything. I just wanted to

get this off my chest, really. Forget I ever said anything, it's probably for the best."

"I don't want to forget a word of what you've just said." My voice is husky and emotional, and I'm surprised to find tears in my eyes.

"You don't." He moves a little closer and I nod and push any nerves aside. "Freddie, I'm not sure why, but I can't stop thinking of you too. When I prayed for a man in Saint Catherine's Chapel, it was your face I saw. When I met you, I immediately felt a connection that surprised me and I couldn't explain. When you were friendly with Kimberly, I burned with jealousy, and every time I was with Alex, I was wishing it was you. What does that mean, Freddie, we are very similar and obviously share the same poor judgement where it concerns our heart but that doesn't matter, all that does is that you feel the same? The trouble is, what are we going to do about it?"

In two steps he is close and as he leans in, his eyes glitter and he growls, "This."

Then he lowers his lips to mine, and it feels like coming home. Kissing Freddie is like the end of something and the beginning of amazing. The flutters, the shivers, the excitement, the passion, all rolled up into one explosive moment of recognition. He's the one, the man of my dreams, the end of the search and the promise of a happy future ahead. The realisation that happy ever afters do exist and dreams do come true. The fireworks are real and explode all around me as I kiss Freddie Carlton back with everything I've got.

Time no longer has any meaning as we share that moment when two souls unite and create magic. We kiss, we touch, and we can't believe our luck that the other feels the same. All our problems and obstacles lay at our feet to be dealt with together, and now I know why people are relentless in their pursuit of love because it's the sweetest treasure.

Then he pulls back and rests his head against mine and stares into my eyes. "So, now it gets interesting."

"It does."

"We have a lot to arrange."

"Such as."

"Our geography for one. If you think I'm letting you go now, you're mistaken. Either you come with me, or I'm moving back to Harpenden to be near you."

"You would do that, for me?"

"I would do *anything* for you, Susie, which reminds me, we're late."

"For what?" I stare at him in confusion because it's 10.30 at night. Late for what?

CHAPTER 37

I'm surprised when Freddie takes my hand and smiles mysteriously. "We have a meeting to attend in Kevin's man cave."

"What about?"

"Something you may find interesting. Come on, let's go and I'll let Kevin explain."

We head down the path and as we turn the corner, I see the wooden cabin nestling in the trees and smell the wood smoke coming from the metal chimney. Freddie squeezes my hand and smiles encouragingly, "Come on, we can't keep them waiting."

"Them?"

He just smiles and knocks on the door and I hear, "Come in."

As we step inside, I look around in astonishment because Kevin is not alone. Sitting on the infamous settee is Lizzie and the Major and beside them is Sandra. Kevin is seated at his desk and two chairs have been set up either side of the log burner, which is throwing out some serious heat. The lamplight creates a cosy atmosphere and I see a tray of what appears to be hot chocolate on the desk that Sandra stands and presents us with. "Here, sit down and grab your drinks before they get cold."

"What's happening?"

I accept the mug gratefully and look at the gathering in surprise as Kevin says in a business-like tone. "We've discovered some information you need to know before this goes any further."

I stare at Freddie who nods and smiles with encouragement before saying softly, "I'm sorry, Suze."

"For what?"

Sandra shakes her head. "Terrible business if you ask me."

"Certainly is, Sandra." Lizzie looks a little upset and I wonder what on earth is going on as Kevin sighs. "You have Lizzie's curiosity to thank for this one, I'm afraid. Maybe she should tell you her story first."

I look at Lizzie and she seems so excited I wonder what she found.

"Well, as soon as you came back with your find, I was interested. I have lived here a long time and never heard anything so romantic, so I made it my business to learn about the history of the ring. Kevin helped me research it on the computer and we discovered that only a few people fitted the description."

"What description?"

She smiles. "The ring could be very expensive, so we researched wealthy individuals of the time. Many were married, so we struck them off and then we found a news item from about fifty years ago that seemed to fit."

Kevin hands me a printed sheet of paper and says kindly, "I printed it out for you, it explains everything."

I stare at the sheet of paper and begin to read the short paragraph.

Local man killed when car skids on ice at Litton Cheney in freezing fog. Thomas Jefferson was killed on Friday late at night as he returned to his home from London. He was pronounced dead at the scene and there were no other parties involved. The car is thought to have slipped on ice and crashed into a tree, killing him outright. Thomas leaves a fiancée Cynthia Adams of this parish but has no other family. The funeral will be announced in due course.

I stare at Freddie in shock. "Isn't that…"

"Yes." He nods sadly. "The man who owned Lake View House."

"So, the ring, his fiancée…"

Sandra interrupts. "Was the owner of the tiffany ring. It's so sad. Lizzie did some digging among her friends…"

"Sandra, this is my story, I'll tell it."

Lizzie looks cross and I stifle a smile as Sandra rolls her eyes. "Well, go on then."

Lizzie's eyes shine as she spills her findings. "Well, Elsie Armitage is such a gossip, and I knew I'd get my information from her. It took me two hours to get past the usual garbage that spills from her mouth, although the story about Robert Jenkins and Violet Cottleshall was particularly juicy…"

"Mother, get to the point." Sandra says with exasperation and Lizzie glares at her. "I was. Settle down, Sandra, and don't use that tone with your mother. Anyway, she told me that she knew a man who knew her gardener and he told her everything."

I'm now getting lost and I'm not the only one judging by the desperate looks being shared around the room, but Lizzie doesn't seem to care and is enjoying her moment in the spotlight.

"Anyway, it seems that poor Cynthia was heartbroken and was left to face things on her own. She never married and she lived as a spinster, never really achieving much and just spending her days working for the good of the community. Well, rumour had it, she never had much, she didn't have a well-paid job and just struggled to make ends meet and the only thing of value in her life was the tiffany ring."

"Why didn't she sell it then? I mean, I feel sorry for her, but surely she would have wanted to make her life more comfortable if she was struggling."

Lizzie shakes her head sadly. "Because it was all she had left of him, the man she loved so hard. She couldn't bear the thought of selling it and wore it every day. Well, maybe she would have changed her mind if she discovered how valuable it is."

I stare at the ring in surprise. "How do you know what it's worth?"

Kevin interrupts. "Well, when Lizzie told me what she had discovered, I had something more to go on. I started delving into public records and the affairs of Thomas Jefferson, most of which are on public record since he was so successful at business. I went through his company documents and assets online and discovered he had registered the purchase of a tiffany ring not long before he died. It was gifted to Cynthia Adams, and the value is astonishing."

I feel my heart beating so madly I wonder if it's about to give out on me and I say slightly breathlessly, "How much?"

"Five hundred thousand pounds."

The silence in the room surrounds me as everyone looks at me with excitement. Five hundred thousand pounds. I stare at the ring and it flashes as it catches the light of the flames from the fire.

Five hundred thousand pounds. It's as if everyone fades away and it's just me and the ring surrounded by its history. The tears form as I picture Cynthia wearing it with pride all her life while she struggled to make ends meet, when she could have lived comfortably. My heart breaks for her as I picture her devastation when she learned of her fiancé's death, and I stare at in disbelief as I remember the moment it fell into my hands. Then I stare at Freddie and we share a moment of understanding. It was always him. It was always Freddie because this ring fell into my hands literally as soon as I met him. The house he was here to view was Thomas Jefferson's and our lives are entwined with theirs.

I want to cry at the pure romance of the occasion and the tragedy of the ring's history and then Sandra says softly, "I'm sorry, Susie, you're not going to like the next bit."

CHAPTER 38

Maybe it was all a dream. My eyes are still tightly shut as my brain wakes and brings back the events that happened yesterday. My first thought is of Freddie and what happened between us. Freddie loves me, well, is on the way to loving me and wants to make a go of it, with *me*. A delicious feeling surrounds me as I remember how I felt at that moment. Nothing else mattered and I can deal with anything life throws at me now because Freddie will be by my side.

I hear a soft groan and smile as the bed dips and Freddie says huskily, "You awake, Suze?"

I open one eye and smile as he peers down at me with a worried look. Then I swallow hard when I see, as usual, he forgot to put on any clothes and stands before me bare chested with tousled hair and a hint of stubble on his face. How did I get so lucky?

"Did you sleep ok after the shock?"

He sits beside me on the bed and looks worried, and I struggle into a sitting position and lean back against the headboard. "I did, actually. I know there was a lot to process but there is nothing I can't deal with – I think."

"Good." For a moment we share a smile and then he looks a little worried. "Are you still ok with *us*, I mean, you haven't had second thoughts in the night, have you?"

I love that he looks so unsure and I grab hold of his hand. "None at all, have you?"

"Of course not but, well, you know, I'm not that lucky in love and I thought you may have had second thoughts now you've slept on it."

For a moment, we just grin stupidly at one another, and I remember how happy we were last night. We still have our barricade in place, but for a while we indulged in a cuddle and a kiss before bedtime. I don't need to rush things with Freddie because we have a lifetime to discover one another, so for now we are content to play this one by the rules, and even though we are sharing a bed, we are not sharing anything else.

I look across at the clock and groan. "It's 9 o'clock already. We should get a move on if we want breakfast and Alex is picking me up at 10 o'clock for our date."

Freddie looks worried. "Are you ok with that?"

"Can't wait, actually."

He nods but looks so miserable I lean closer and kiss him softly on the lips. "Don't worry, I'll be fine. We'll just stick to the plan and hopefully it will all be over by teatime."

"I'm not sure it will be that easy. What if something goes wrong?"

"What could go wrong, Freddie, we hold all the cards?"

He nods and heads into the bathroom, and I take the time to think about the most damaging part of the story last night. Thank God for Lizzie and Kevin, they may have just saved my future.

It feels strange at breakfast because the guys had an early start at their convention and they will be heading home afterwards. I didn't even get a chance to say goodbye properly, but at least we are all friends on Facebook now, so it never seems that final. I am looking forward to seeing their photos and can't wait to bug them with mine, especially the funny ones I spend way too long laughing at every day. Eloise and Greg are still here, although they are leaving this morning, and when we head inside the room, Eloise smiles brightly.

"Hey guys, it's our last day. You know, the time has gone so quickly, I can't believe it."

Greg nods. "Yes, we've really enjoyed it though and have booked to come next year already. What about you, when are you off?"

"Tomorrow." Freddie shakes his head sadly. "Although I could be tempted to extend it a few days, but Sandra told me they are fully booked. They nearly always are, which doesn't surprise me."

Eloise looks at me and smiles. "And you, Susie, will you be heading home, or has a certain police officer persuaded you to stay?"

"No, nothing like that, I'm heading home."

"With a valuable addition, you lucky thing."

We all look at the ring sparkling on my finger and I feel a little protective of it. It surely deserves its own happy ever after and I'm not sure if I'm up to the job. I feel so much pressure to live happily ever after, but so much depends on that, not least my relationship with Freddie. Will he hate me after a few weeks when he discovers how methodical I am when it comes to lists and planning? Will he hate my colour coordinated wardrobe and labelled drawers? Will he despair over my well-ordered cupboards and baulk at the list of to do items I tick off my list every day?

I glance across at him and worry about our future. Will

this work, where will we live and how can we make happy ever after happen?

Greg hands me his business card. "If you change your mind about that story, give me a call. It could help make you a mini celebrity. Stranger things have happened."

"Thanks." I smile and pocket the card. "I may just take you up on that offer."

Once again, we enjoy Sandra's award winning breakfast and yet my heart is heavy. I just need to get through today and then we can start our lives, Freddie and me, two identical souls tied together for eternity, or at least until one of us messes it up.

Freddie seems wrapped in his own thoughts, and I know he's worried. "It will be ok, you know." I smile at him reassuringly and he rakes his fingers through his hair. "I hope so, I would hate for anything to go wrong."

"I'm not sure it could, we covered every angle last night – I think."

He nods and then smiles sweetly. "Are you happy, Suze?"

"I will be, Freddie, are you?"

"I will be."

We share a smile and my heart settles. Yes, we'll be happy – together and I don't need Lolita Sharples to tell me that.

CHAPTER 39

Alex is waiting in his usual spot, and I have to admit, he is one handsome man. I feel a little sad that it's come to this and wonder if he'll be happy sometime in the future – despite everything, I hope he is.

He moves across and takes me in his arms and whispers, "I missed you, at least we have the whole day and night together."

"What do you mean, night, Alex?" I stare at him in confusion and he smiles cheekily. "Well, I hoped we could spend a little longer together as it's not long before you leave. I've taken the liberty of booking us a table reservation at the local pub and then thought we could relax at mine afterwards. I want to spend as long as possible together, I hate that you're going home tomorrow."

He kisses me softly and I pull back quickly, feeling bad at the surprise in his eyes.

"We should go, I really want to see what you have planned."

I smile to cover up the fact I didn't want to kiss him, and he just nods and opens my door.

"My lady." He laughs softly and heads around to the driver's side, and we are soon pulling out of the driveway.

For the next hour, we just drive and he points out various landmarks and places of interest and yet I can't really appreciate them because I'm suddenly wondering if this could all go badly wrong. Alex seems like such a nice guy and I can't really believe what I heard last night, but then again, you can still be a nice guy, even if you are a desperate one.

At precisely 11 o'clock, I say quickly, "I don't suppose we could stop by the Frog and Lily; I think I left my jacket there the other day and have been meaning to go and get it."

He looks surprised. "Of course, it's not far. Maybe we could grab a snack and a drink there while we're at it."

"Sounds great."

My stomach is in knots as I count the minutes before we get there. This could go badly wrong and I hate doing things like this. In fact, I've always shied away from confrontation, but this time I have no choice.

Even the beautiful scenery goes unnoticed as we speed along the country lanes, and my heart is racing faster than the car at this point. Alex hums along to the music and doesn't appear to have a care in the world as the little red sports car eats up the miles to judgement day.

We arrive soon enough and my heart flutters when I see some familiar cars in the car park. This is really happening and this may be my last chance to stop it. If I had my way, I would have just headed home and blocked his calls, but the others wouldn't hear of it. They told me it was my public duty to see this through and yet now it's happening, I am having second, third and fourth thoughts. I can't do this.

"Is everything ok, Susie, you've gone quiet on me."

"Sorry." I smile brightly and laugh self-consciously. "I suppose I'm a bit tired, the sea air really knocks me out, I'm never normally like this."

"Yes, it does have a habit of doing that. Never mind, I'll look after you."

He grins and I feel bad all over again. What am I doing?

~

WE HEAD INSIDE and I swallow hard when I see them all sitting at a table overlooking the garden and I catch Freddie's eye and notice he looks as worried as I am. Kimberly smiles as we approach the bar and Alex says gallantly, "I don't suppose anyone's handed in a jacket, my girlfriend left it here a few days ago."

His girlfriend! My heart sinks and I shuffle awkwardly on the spot, locked in a miserable madness. This is so complicated, which shouldn't surprise me because complicated should be my middle name and I don't suppose I will ever learn.

"You're in luck, we've got it out the back. Are you staying for a drink, I can fetch them first and then bring it over?"

"Yes, and some food if you're serving."

Kimberly nods and hands him two menus and signals the table just around the corner from the others. "If you want to sit over there, I'll come and take your order."

Alex orders us a couple of drinks and we head across and take our seats, and my heart rate quickens to near death levels. This is it.

I think I count down in my mind until she returns and Alex reaches out and takes my hand in his and looks at the ring.

"You know, every time I see that ring, it reminds me how special this is. Have you ever considered getting it valued?"

"Not really, I'm guessing it's worth a lot, but to be honest, I'm thinking on that offer of going to the press."

I note the alarm in his eyes and my heart sinks. "I wouldn't advise you to do that."

"Why not?"

I stare at him with a blank expression and he shakes his head. "It wouldn't end well. The press are like vultures. They would delve into your past and even though I know your job is perfectly acceptable, by the time they finish, you would be a scarlet woman. Then they would question whether you are a deserving recipient of the ring and it could all blow up in your face."

"But that wouldn't matter because I'm not thinking of keeping the ring." The look on his face says it all, and he stutters, "Why ever not?"

"I don't know, Alex, I feel bad about the whole thing. It's too valuable to keep, and I feel like a thief. If anything, the chapel could benefit from the sale and it would help keep the monument for generations in the future to enjoy. I don't need it, not really. How can you need something you've never had?"

He takes my hand in his and looks me straight in the eye. "Now listen to me, don't do anything you may regret. Don't make any decisions based on the future of this ring before you've had time to think them through carefully. If you decide to sell, then I can arrange that for you but I wouldn't trust just anyone with this. There are a lot of unscrupulous people out there and I should know."

"Why?"

"Why what?"

"Why should you know?"

"Because I'm a police officer, of course, I meet them every day."

He sighs and takes a sip of his soda water and says with a slight edge to his voice, "Promise me, no press and no sale, not yet until you've had time to think about it."

"Alex."

We look up and I watch the blood drain from his face as he whispers, "Donna."

I look with interest at the pretty girl who is looking at him with venom in her eyes and he wilts under the force of it.

"What are you doing here, I thought…"

"That I was on holiday in Ibiza - wrong. What I want to know is what the hell is going on and why are you holding that woman's hand?"

He drops my hand as if it burns and says falteringly, "But…when did you get back?"

"This morning, I grabbed a cab from the airport because I decided to return a day earlier than planned. Call me stupid, but I was desperate to see my fiancé."

She looks at me with a hard look and I shrink back in my seat and then look at Alex in surprise, "Alex, what's going on?"

"Um, listen, Susie, maybe I can deal with this outside, I just need a word with Donna."

He almost jumps from his seat and drags the poor woman outside, and I lean back and shake my head. "Well, that was intense."

Freddie looks around the corner and says with concern, "Are you ok, you did very well, I must say."

"Yes, darling, not a word out of place." Sandra nods her approval and Kevin whispers, "Shh, if we're quiet, we may be able to hear them."

We all look outside and see Alex and Donna arguing in the car park and she is pointing at his car angrily.

Lizzie laughs as Kimberly comes over to take a look. "I hope she annihilates the creep."

I look at her in surprise and she shrugs. "As soon as Freddie told me about Alex, I knew I couldn't keep quiet. It's well known around here that he's engaged to Donna. They've been together since school."

She turns to me and smiles ruefully. "That car, the house he probably took you to, they're all hers and I expect this will be the last straw because this isn't the first time he's cheated on her."

We look with interest as they continue arguing and Sandra sighs. "Such a shame, they look like such a lovely couple. She doesn't deserve the trouble he brings on her."

We nod because apparently cheating is the least of their problems.

Kimberly hisses, "He's coming back, pretend we haven't seen anything."

As Donna heads off in the sports car, I wonder what story he will fabricate now and lean back and watch him enter the pub looking sheepish.

He heads across and the others look away as if they never saw a thing, and he sighs as he slides back into the seat opposite.

"I'm sorry about that, Susie. Donna just won't accept we're over. She's done this before, made a scene when she's seen me with another girl, and I'm worried about her mental health, really. I should try to help her, but I only ever make things worse and she does it again."

He takes my hands and his eyes shine with unbridled emotion. "I'm so sorry, what must you think of me?"

"Um, Alex."

"Yes, Susie."

"It appears that Donna has stolen your car."

He looks over his shoulder and nods. "It's fine, I gave her the keys and told her to go to her parents. I'll collect the car later. I should have given her a lift, but I didn't want to leave you. I expect her father will bring it back. If not, we can get a cab back to your place and pick up your car."

"I must say you seem very calm about this, Alex. That was quite upsetting really."

He smiles. "I'm used to it, so I didn't think anything of it. I'm sorry, you must think it's all a little strange, it's just that, well, Donna has emotional problems, which is another reason why I didn't want to go to the press. She would be triggered and who knows what fabricated lies she would tell them. I'm sorry, Susie, you didn't deserve to experience that."

Kimberly heads over and takes our order, which gives me a moment to collect my thoughts. I could almost believe Alex. He is so convincing and for the first time, I feel a little doubt. Maybe Kimberly was wrong and Donna just told her the story because she is unhinged. Perhaps we are judging Alex harshly and have got this all wrong.

CHAPTER 40

The next thirty minutes are made up of polite conversation and long silences. Unlike the ones with Freddie, they are not comfortable silences and I feel so on edge I almost can't eat.

After a while, Alex takes my hand in his, running his thumb over the ring and smiles. "Let's not allow Donna to spoil what we have. The legend of this ring was right about one thing."

"Which part?"

"That the first person you meet would be your future. We can't argue with that because look at us now."

"Excuse me, young man."

We look up as Lizzie hovers at the edge of the table and looks at him sharply and I'm not sure if he even recognises her from when she groped his leg the day he came to Happy Ever After.

"I'm sorry, but you're talking about the legend of the ring of Saint Catherine's, aren't you?"

He looks a little surprised. "How do you know about that?"

"Look at me, I'm old, I know everything."

Lizzie laughs and I stifle a grin as Alex looks confused. "But..."

"You see, young man, I think you've got it wrong."

Alex looks a little pale and says weakly, "I don't think..."

Lizzie sits down beside me and fixes him with a stern look. "You see, I know that the ring was placed there around thirty years ago by a woman named Cynthia Adams. She was engaged to a very wealthy man who died in a car crash one day."

"Yes, that's right."

Alex nods and looks at me apologetically as he struggles to deal with the overbearing woman who is taking no prisoners. "You see, the woman placed the ring in the chapel for a reason. She wanted it to answer the prayers of a deserving woman who went to pray for a husband. According to the historical society in Abbotsbury, a note she left was found in her belongings when she died. She wanted the power of Saint Catherine to find a home for her pride and joy and where better than the place she was set to marry her one true love. However, there was nothing in the letter about a legend involving that man being the first one she met since finding the ring. Care to explain yourself, young man."

Alex shrugs. "Well, I heard differently. I asked a local historian myself who told me about the second part, so we may never know who is correct."

"I'm sorry, son, but I do."

Kevin stops by and Alex looks even more surprised as Kevin says bluntly, "I contacted the head office of Saint Catherines when Susie found the ring and they informed me they would look into it. I heard back from them yesterday morning. Apparently, there was a file lodged with them that was a copy of the last will and testament of Cynthia Adams. It stated that if a diamond tiffany ring was ever declared found by a woman who prayed for a man, she was to be allowed to keep the ring. She gave details of the solicitor they needed to inform who would verify her ownership. There was nothing in the letter about meeting a man, I'm not sure where you got your facts from."

Alex is now looking furious and I shrivel in my seat as he says angrily, "Well, I only know what I heard and what I feel. You see none of it matters because I love Susie and she loves me. We are going to be together and have the ring to thank for us meeting in the first place. Now, if you'll excuse me, I think we should be leaving because we are trying to enjoy our last day together."

"You've got that right."

Freddie stands up and now there is quite a crowd around the table.

"Ok, tell me." Alex sighs heavily. "You may as well say your piece too because I'm starting to see the picture here."

He looks at me and says apologetically. "Obviously these people don't approve of us and are trying to put doubts in your mind. I'm not sure what their agenda is, but whatever it is, isn't worth hearing. Come on, let's leave them to their wild imaginations and try to enjoy our day."

Freddie shakes his head. "It *is* your last day together because I'm guessing as soon as Susie hears what you're really after, she won't give you the time of day."

"Oh, let me guess, the unwelcome roommate. This is all a little sad if you ask me. You want her for yourself, probably because you see an opportunity here and as for you." He looks at Lizzie and Kevin. "You should get your facts right first. Now, I am fast losing my cool and even if you are right and I am wrong, what does it matter, anyway? We are still going to keep in touch regardless, and if that means we fall in love and live happily ever after, then that's what fate intended in the first place. Now, if you'll excuse me."

"I'm sorry, sir, your card was declined, do you have any other form of payment, cash perhaps?"

Kimberly looks at him apologetically and then winks as she turns to look at me.

"But..." Alex looks confused. "Are you sure, maybe it's the signal, can you try again please?"

Kimberly shakes her head. "I'm sorry. It told me to keep the card. You will need to contact your bank; you can use our phone if you like."

Alex jumps up. "Fine, where can I make the call?"

He makes to walk away and Sandra jumps up. "You know, I was certain I had seen you somewhere before and now I know."

"Oh great, another one." Alex shakes his head because it must be pretty obvious right now that he's been set up. "Well, you may not know this, but I'm an avid reader of the Dorset Gazette and I'm always poring over the pages and sifting through the editorial with a fine-tooth comb."

"You should get a life." Alex is fast losing his cool and Sandra looks at Kevin. "Do you remember when you asked me what I'd do if I went bankrupt and didn't tell you?"

"Of course, you told me you'd kick me out and run away with the gardener."

Lizzie laughs. "That's my girl."

Sandra turns to Alex. You see, Kevin is always looking for problems to solve and as it happened, that question came at just the right time because I remembered reading about an Alex Murphy of Weymouth who had filed for bankruptcy. It wasn't that long ago either, which is why the incident was fresh in my mind. Anyway, I didn't think that much about it until Kimberly came to visit one night."

She looks at the barmaid, who frowns. "Yes, they were telling me all about Susie and the amazing ring and told me she had met her Prince Charming, Alex Murphy, no less.

Well, I was surprised because the only police officer I'd heard of called Alex Murphy, was currently engaged to a friend of my sister's. Apparently, he had lost his home and was living with her."

She turns to me and says sadly, "Even that car was hers. You see, he has nothing. I thought it suspect when Sandra and Kevin told me your story so I called my sister. She was surprised and said for all she knew, they were still together but she would text her and find out. Well, as it turns out, she thought they were still engaged and was heading home early to confront him. So, that led us to wonder what he was playing at."

She looks at Alex and shakes her head. "It has to be the ring. You knew the value of it and decided that was your way out of financial ruin. All you had to do was to convince Susie you were made for each other and then when you were a couple, you could persuade her to sell the ring and split the proceeds. That's why you didn't want any publicity because Donna would find out and spill your secret. I'm right, aren't I?"

Alex looks like a deer caught in headlights and appears to have lost the power of speech. He looks at me helplessly and then at the stern faces surrounding him.

I'm not sure why I feel so sorry for him but somehow, I do and say softly, "Come on, let's get some air."

I reach out and take his hand and lead him from the pub and as the air hits us outside, he says gratefully, "Thanks for that, things were getting a little out of hand in there."

"It's fine, I'm sorry, Alex, that was tough."

"Do you hate me, Susie?"

I know I should but I don't and say sadly, "No, I don't hate you but I don't like you very much at the moment. For what it's worth, I'd already decided this wasn't what I wanted anyway and was going to end it yesterday as it happens.

Then Freddie and the others told me your story, and I suppose I had to know for myself."

"So, what now?"

"Nothing. I'll return home and you'll try to repair your relationship, I guess. I am sorry that you lost your money, but this was never going to be the answer. You'll get through it; you have a job and a woman who may need some persuading to stay, but I'm sure you can convince her. What I want to know is why you went bankrupt in the first place? You have a good job, you're young, what happened?"

"Life happened, Susie and I wanted everything. I wanted the nice house, nice car, holidays and latest gadgets. I thought I was invincible. One loan led to another, then one credit card multiplied several times, and I was soon spent up to the maximum. I was drowning in debt and used credit cards to pay my monthly mortgage payments. My food was also gained that way, and soon the repayments were more than I earned. I suppose I couldn't see a way out of it, and even Donna doesn't know the full extent. How can I marry her when I have nothing to give? I can't even pay for a wedding, and she will hate me when she discovers how bad I am at money management. Not much of a catch now, am I?"

He looks so destroyed my heart aches for him, and I suppose I forgive him a little.

I take his hand and lead him over to one of the tables in the beer garden and as we sit side by side, I say gently. "Put this behind you, Alex, and go and seek help. Many people have money troubles, many people lose it all, but they can start again. It won't be easy, but as soon as you have a plan to follow, you can start to rebuild your life. Be better than this and make this count as a lesson learned that sets you on the right path. You'll be fine, I just know it, and five years from now, I'm guessing you will have turned a corner and will look back on this as the day your life began."

"I'm sorry Susie, I feel even worse now you're so understanding."

"I'm no one to judge. I go from one bad decision to another most of the time. I have a career that's unconventional and I'm not sure what I'll do to replace it. I have no life plan and let fate make my decisions for me. I was only too happy to believe your story because I am that gullible. The thing is, it was all staring me in the face because I did find my happy ever after here. He was already waiting when I arrived."

"Freddie?"

"Yes." I smile at the thought of him waiting anxiously inside, and Alex smiles. "I'm glad. In fact, you are richer than me in every way, but perhaps the only one that counts. You have friends, someone who loves you, and an attitude to life that's addictive. I'm sorry for dragging you into my mess, but just for the record, if things were different, I would be pursuing the hell out of you."

He sighs heavily and reaches inside his jacket pocket. "Listen, I have some cash, take it and pay for the meal. If it's ok with you, I think I'll walk to the nearest police station and grab a lift back to see if I can smooth things over with Donna."

"No need, I'll pay this time, after all, it is my turn."

"But…"

"No buts, Alex, let me help in just this small way."

"You're a great person, Susie."

"And so are you. You know, you shouldn't feel bad about what happened. Losing control invokes desperation which leads to momentary insanity. But that's all it is, a moment in time that will soon be replaced with another and we can only hope the replacement is a better one. Now get out of here and prove it is and I hope it all works out."

He hesitates for a moment and then, to my surprise, leans

in and kisses me softly on the cheek, whispering, "Be happy, Susie. I have a feeling you have found everything you were looking for, and if anyone deserves that ring, it's you."

I watch him walk away with a mixture of sadness and relief. Poor Alex, he will have a mountain to climb and I hope he makes it.

"Are you ok?"

I look up and see a worried Freddie hovering nearby, and I smile brightly. "I am, actually. Come on, Freddie, let's go and get a drink, I certainly need one after that."

He takes my hand and I follow him inside to spend time with the most amazing people I have ever met. Whatever tomorrow brings can surely be nowhere near as dramatic as today.

CHAPTER 41

We head back to Happy Ever After and once we have dissected the entire confrontation in great detail, everyone drifts back to their normal pastimes.

Lizzie decided that the Major had slept in long enough and was in the mood, whatever that meant and Sandra had beds to strip and laundry waiting in preparation for her next guests. Kevin was on gardening duty and Kimberly reluctantly had to head back to the Frog and Lily to relieve the manager, although she looked quite excited about that.

Freddy decided we should take a long walk along the cliff edge, and so we set out to endure a marathon session in the wild.

This time as we walk, Freddie's hand is planted firmly in mine and we steal many kisses along the way. The sun is high in the sky and the seagulls are calling out for their next meal. The sea is calm as if after a raging storm and it certainly feels that way as we stroll along the strip of land that separates land from ocean and talk long and hard about what happened and how we can make this work.

"You know, you could always come and stay with me in Guildford. You can have your own room if you like, you'll probably need one for your luggage alone."

I can't help but laugh. "Only if you promise to build a barricade down the middle, you keep to your half and me to mine."

"Yes, that could work, I've been looking for a live in for a while now."

"You have?"

He nods seriously. "It would be handy to have a spider catcher on hand. I would insist that was your job, the rest I'm happy to cope with myself."

"I'm sorry, Freddie, you are pushing me a step too far. We may have to renegotiate out terms. I mean, I'm happy to escort you to functions and act as your plus one, after all, it is what I'm trained for but the wildlife, I'm sorry, that is a step too far."

He smiles and pulls me close. "Would you really move in with me?" He looks serious with is unlike him, and I suddenly feel a little shy.

"I may be tempted if I think it's worth my while."

He leans in and kisses me softly at first and then deeper, and I find my toes curl and my heart sings as I realise how good love feels. I'm in no doubt I love Freddie already. It may not have been love at first sight, but it's close. I think Polly and Miles always knew we would be perfect for one another; they are the people who know us best after all and I have to hand it to them, I think they were spot on and I thank God for my best friend and her boyfriend in intervening in my life in such a spectacular way.

I'm not sure how long we walk for, but by the time we return to Happy Ever After, we have talked long and hard about the future – our future.

I will visit Freddie in Gomshall on alternate weeks and he

will come to Slipend on the other. He will stay with his parents at first because they only live in Harpenden, unless of course our relationship accelerates a little.

I'm not sure who we are kidding really because I'm pretty certain he won't spend one night at his parents, but it felt good to have a plan in place so there were no presumptions on either part.

I feel so happy as we head back through the rickety gate leading from the beach and am surprised when I see Sandra racing towards us.

"Oh, there you are, you have a visitor. He's been waiting at least an hour and may not have long."

"What do you mean?"

"Lizzie's entertaining him, you had better be quick."

She shakes her head and we follow her none the wiser as to who it is. I'm half expecting to see Alex and I wonder how I would feel about that, but despite everything, I hope he works things out and moves on from his problems.

However, the man waiting nervously beside Lizzie, who is invading his personal space so happily, is a man I've never seen before. He is wearing a suit and perching a briefcase on his knee, fidgeting with his tie as Lizzie sniffs his neck.

Sandra says loudly, "Lizzie, come and help me with the baking."

"Since when did you need help with baking, I thought you were a geriatric version of Nigella?"

"Now, mother!"

Lizzie slides off her seat and grumbles, "How many more times must I tell you to call me Lizzie, mother sounds so old and quite frankly, Sandra, most people would think it was the other way around. I mean, for goodness' sake, throw away your Marks and Spencer card and grab one from River Island instead, you are sooo old before your time."

She continues to berate her daughter's fashion sense as

she follows her out of the room, and the man looks so relieved it makes me want to laugh.

He looks up and smiles. "You must be Susie, hi, I'm Mr Cartwright from Cartwright, Grimes, Sanderson and sons. Sorry it's such a mouthful but we've added more partners along the way and knowing us, it will not stop there."

He looks at Freddie and nods respectfully. "Mr Carlton, I presume. We spoke on the phone."

Freddie looks puzzled. "Yes, but that was ages ago, I wasn't aware we had arranged a meeting."

He turns to me and says, "Mr Cartwright is the solicitor handling the sale of Lake View. Before I came here, I called him to discuss the details of the purchase. At the time I was only looking for a new project and when Miles learned I would be heading this way, he suggested staying here."

"I see." We share a smile and I roll my eyes. "Which was the perfect opportunity for Polly to book me into the same hotel as a gift for my birthday. It all begins to make more sense now."

Mr Cartwright nods. "Yes, I am responsible for the sale of Lake View but that's not why I'm here, unless..."

He looks at Freddie hopefully and Freddie looks torn.

"I'm still thinking about it. To be honest, it's a lot to think about. The place needs serious work, almost a complete rebuild, and it's so far from my family, I'm not sure I would settle. It's a little remote and despite how much I love it, I'm not sure I could afford the renovation. However, the money would be easily raised by a few investors should I decide to proceed, but I need more time."

Mr Cartwright nods. "Of course, you know where I am."

He turns to me. "It was you I came to see, Miss Mahoney."

"Me?" I feel nervous and the ring feels tight on my finger. "Is it about the ring, do I have to give it back?"

He shakes his head before saying gently, "May I take a look."

I make to take the ring off but he interrupts, "On your finger, if I may."

It feels a little strange offering my hand to a total stranger, and I cast a look at Freddie who is looking interested.

"Well, I never really expected to see this with my own eyes. You are very lucky, Miss Mahoney."

He studies the ring and I feel a little smug as I look at the sparkling diamond. "I am."

I share a smile with Freddie because the ring is not why I feel so lucky, *he* is and I would trade this ring for a lifetime with him.

The solicitor looks up and nods. "Well, you will pleased to know that I am also acting on behalf of the late Cynthia Adams, the original recipient of the ring, which was purchased by my also late client, Thomas Jefferson. I have with me the necessary paperwork to assign ownership to you and you will be pleased to know that it's yours to keep and do with what you like."

He rummages in his briefcase and removes a manila folder, from which he pulls out several sheets of paper. He hands it to me and says professionally. "Take your time to look over it, but it's merely to say that you are the heir to Cynthia Adam's estate."

"I'm sorry, did you say, estate?"

I stare at him in surprise and he nods. "Yes, like Mr Jefferson, Cynthia had no dependants or relatives to leave her estate to. She decided to make it interesting and drew up her last will and testament around the ring. Once the ring had an owner, the rest would follow. As I said before, you are a very lucky young lady because that person is you."

"But…" I stare at him in astonishment, and he laughs. "Enjoy your good fortune, my dear, because you have it all."

"But I thought she had no money. I was told she lived frugally and struggled to meet ends meet."

Mr Cartwright looks surprised. "There's a big difference to having no money and living frugally. Cynthia chose to live way below her means because that was how she wanted it. She was actually very wealthy in her own right. She came from a family who had rather a large fortune and, being their only child, inherited the lot. She chose to invest her money rather than spend it and died leaving it all in trust to benefit a woman she felt a kinship with. From what I know about Cynthia, she was an admirable woman. She didn't conform and chose to live her life the way she wanted to. She was never one to do as she should, she did what she wanted. She may have lost the only man she loved, but she made her life count. You should do your research on her, I'm sure you would find her a very interesting person indeed."

Freddie interrupts. "So, let me get this straight, Susie inherits the lot, whatever that is."

"Yes. The stocks, the shares, the properties she rented out and the ring. You may need a solicitor of your own, my dear, I think you're going to need one."

I'm not sure when Mr Cartwright left. I'm not sure when the day turned to night and I'm not sure how long I sit for in the chair overlooking the garden. The only thing I'm sure about is that I am living in a dream. Things like this don't happen to me. To anyone. This isn't real life; this is the stuff of fairy tales. It's only when Freddie crouches before me and holds my face in his hands, looking so concerned that I blink and the tears come.

He whispers, "Come on, you need to eat and get an early night. Maybe a drink will help, I'm sure I need one."

"Is it true, Freddie, what Mr Cartwright said?"

"I think it is. I bet you never saw that one coming."

He grins and a sob/giggle makes its way from somewhere inside and as his arms close around me and pull me tight, I know more than anything else, he is my happy ever after.

EPILOGUE

THREE YEARS LATER

My heart flutters, my nerves are right on the edge and my mind is scrambled. I hold on to Polly's arm and take a few deep breaths and try to keep my emotions in check.

"Are you ok, Suze?"

Polly looks concerned as I brush a tear away and my lower lip trembles. "I'm not sure."

She squeezes my arm with a reassurance I badly need right now and smiles through her own tears.

"I'm so happy for you, I can't believe this is really happening."

"Me neither."

We stand facing the open doorway and only the flicker of firelight lights our way as I take a deep breath and feel the chill of the evening breeze make my dress rustle.

"You look beautiful, Suze."

"So do you, Polly." For a moment we just stare at each other, not daring to speak. There's a hush in the air that wraps the occasion in suspense.

Then with a deep breath, I say in as firm a voice as I can muster, "We should really go inside now."

"Of course."

Polly smiles and I almost lose it again, but I settle my nerves and look down for reassurance. My tiffany ring shines like a beacon of hope in a darkening landscape, and I smile. "This is for you, Cynthia."

I raise it and kiss the stone, my tears splashing on the rarest treasure.

As I turn to the south doorway of the chapel of dreams, I feel the steady beat of my heart, reminding me how important this moment is.

The music fills my ears, and a shiver passes through me at the sound of the haunting melody. Fairy lights adorn the ancient space as the wind whips through the chapel, causing me to shiver a little. Large lanterns holding church candles line my route, and wild flowers and greenery decorate the crumbling ruin.

As I grasp my bouquet of tulips and hyacinths, I swallow hard and prepare for the dream to reach a happy conclusion. This time there *will* be a ceremony at Saint Catherine's Chapel, and the ring will fulfil the role it was always meant to.

As I step inside, I blink away the tears and smile at the man waiting so patiently before the large glass window. Beside him, his brother stands looking so proud of his younger brother and new bride, who accompanies me down the aisle.

The priest stands watching me approach, and he beams with happiness and as the music plays softly, I begin the short walk to marry the man I prayed to find on this very spot.

I am certain Saint Catherine is standing shoulder to shoulder with Thomas Jefferson and Cynthia Adams as they watch their legend reach its conclusion. I am pretty certain they would approve of our journey, and I hope we have done them proud.

The only other life in the darkening chapel are the flames from the candles dancing against the breeze and the spiders that are sure to be plotting to ruin our special day from the cracks in the stone walls.

The rest of our guests are waiting elsewhere for the party to begin, but this was always going to be our special moment where the four of us finished the journey we set out on three years to the day I found the ring.

As I take the short walk to join my bridegroom, I note the emotion in his eyes. When Freddie asked me to marry him, it was on that very spot. Before the huge window in the place that has come to mean so much. My answer was always going to be yes, there was never any question of that and as I hoped for all those years ago, I found my soul mate in this ancient monument like so many before me.

He smiles as I reach his side, and I blink back the tears as he takes my hands. We stand facing each other as we declare our love before the intimate gathering. Simple and sweet was always going to be our theme because, after all, that's all we wanted.

When the time came to leave Happy Ever After, we did so with a heavy heart. The place had woven its magic into our hearts, so it was no surprise that we bought Lake View House inside of three months of leaving and rented a little cottage nearby while Freddie worked hard to create a masterpiece. I think these past three years have been the happiest of my life as we set up home together and planned our future.

Now we work side by side, as I organise my soon to be husband and run his office. Freddie is good at what he does and is in huge demand as many people refurbish the homes of the past and bring them into the future.

We are no exception, and with Cynthia's money and Freddie's barn sale, we have managed the impossible. Lake View is finished and all of our family and friends are currently waiting there for us to arrive as husband and wife.

The priest turns to Freddie and says softly, "You have something to say to your bride."

Freddie nods and the romantic glow of the fairy lights illuminate his face as he stares at me with pure emotion. "Susie Mahoney, I love you. I never thought I would get my happy ending, but I found it with you. Fate brought us together, and it didn't take a legend, or magic of the past to make me realise almost immediately that I never wanted to let you go. You are my match in every way and I couldn't imagine life without you. If I could change one thing about you, it would be your strange fear of spiders."

He winks and I roll my eyes and then his voice softens and he whispers, "I love you, darling, and am definitely the happiest man alive right now as I dedicate my love to you. I promise you that our love will only burn brighter over time because if I'm sure of anything, it's that we were always meant to be together. I cannot find enough words to describe all the love I have in my heart for you. It's not just physical either, it's the coming together of souls. Love is a word that is used far too often that could never describe the fierce, infinite and blazing passion that I have in my heart for you. You are a million dreams come true. You are kind, intelligent, witty and you make me look at the world as if seeing it for the first time. You acknowledge my strengths and accept my flaws. You make me want to be a better person every day. I take you as you are now, tomorrow and for eternity to come, to be my wife. Even when we have created a thousand memories, I promise to always see you with the same eyes and the same heart that I see you with at this exact moment. So today, I vow to honour, respect you, support you and encourage you. I promise to dream with you, celebrate with you, and walk beside you through whatever life brings. I vow to laugh with you and comfort you during times of joy and times of sorrow. I promise to always pursue you, to fight for you, and love you unconditionally and wholeheartedly for the rest of my life. You are my best friend and I'm the luckiest man on Earth to call you my wife."

There are no words to describe how much his words mean to me, and it takes me a moment to realise that I must deliver my own words that came so naturally when I thought about what I would say.

Smiling through my tears, I squeeze his hand and say softly, "Freddie Carlton, you came into my life uninvited, and it didn't take me long to realise I never wanted you to leave. From that first moment you weaved your magic around my heart, I was lost to you forever. I'm so proud to become your wife. I love the way you always finish my sentences and understand the crazy world inside my head and always make me smile when I feel like crying when yet another thing goes wrong with our renovation. I love that you always reach for my hand whenever we walk and share your kisses at the most inappropriate times. I love that you're open to trying new things and make me question my sanity every minute of the day. Today, I want to make promises to you that I will always keep. I promise to never stop holding your hand. I promise to give you all the love and support that you deserve and to keep you organised, despite all your attempts to use the floor as a filing cabinet. I promise to stand by your side while you face the world, and I will try to promise to listen when you speak. If life darkens, I want to hold the light to show you the way, or sit with you in the shadows. I promise to grow alongside you, but also to never grow up. I promise to love, respect, protect and trust you, and give you the best of myself, for I know that together we will build a life far better than either of us could imagine alone. I choose you. I'll choose you over and over and over, without pause, without doubt, I'll keep choosing you. Today is the beginning of an amazing journey, but I already belong to you. Falling in love with you wasn't falling at all—it was walking into a house and knowing I was home Did I say that I loved you despite your weird fear of spiders? We built our own castle, but not on the sand. Ours has much stronger foundations than that, gifted to us by two people who loved so hard but never had the chance to fulfil their dreams. We have that chance and we will never let them down. Did I say I love you?" I smile and step closer and look into his eyes that are brimming with emotion. "I will never stop and that is my promise to you."

Freddie nods and I see his eyes glistening with tears as he repeats the sacred vows the priest instructs him to repeat after him. Then I do the same before Miles steps forward and hands Freddie the ring that we chose together. I love the way he slips it on my finger and it joins the ring that has brought us so much good fortune. Now the ring has its own companion to travel through life with, and I have mine. A happy ending from a tragic beginning, and as the priest says softly, "I now declare you husband and wife, you may now kiss your bride." Freddie wastes no time at all in pulling me close and whispers, "Our first kiss as husband and wife, I promise you many more every day for the rest of our lives."

Our first kiss as a married couple feels different somehow. The same flutters, the same fireworks and the same love in my heart, but now there's a commitment that we have made before God in this magical place. It feels as if we have met at a crossroads and joined hands to walk the rest of the way through life – together. It feels like home.

EPILOGUE 2

It feels good as we walk down the hill to the waiting car. Freddie holds my hand and I try not to imagine the state of my white satin shoes as they navigate the sheep's gifts that are littered over the hill. Miles and Polly walk behind us, hand in hand, and it must look a strange sight to the tourists who have been denied access to the monument for the past hour. A few call out their congratulations and I feel like a celebrity as we reach the bottom of the hill to find Kevin waiting with his Kirrin wagon that has doubled as a wedding car for the journey.

Not the most luxurious of wedding vehicles, but a memorable one and he beams as we approach.

"Congratulations, well done, and all that nonsense. You know, as a happily married man myself, I can tell you will make it through. To be honest, Sandra and I have never considered divorce in all the years we've been married, murder perhaps, but never divorce."

He winks as we laugh at the astonishment on Polly and Miles's faces because quite frankly, Kevin is the strangest man I think we will ever meet.

We bundle inside the Kirrin wagon and Polly says happily, "That was beautiful and way more memorable than a full church and a truckload of guests. Thank you so much for asking us to witness that, I wouldn't have missed it for the world."

I smile through my tears because it appears I'm an emotional wreck right now and Polly laughs. "Stop crying, Suze, you'll make my mascara run and how will that look in the photographs?"

Kevin pipes up, "I think Liam got some good ones, you know that man is a maestro with the camera."

Liam is Kevin's son-in-law and a photographer for Vogue. As soon as they learned of our wedding, Sandra and Kevin insisted they pay for the photographer as a wedding gift. I'm not sure if any money actually changed hands, but that's not the point because Liam is the nicest and most talented man you could ever meet. He has sped off to be at Lake View before we get there, and I am looking forward to seeing what magic he has created.

"So, now you're married, Freddie can let his guard slip a little and you will soon realise what an idiot you married. Bad luck, Suze, I did try to warn you."

Miles grins as Freddie shrugs. "I think Susie knew that already."

He reaches for the bottle of champagne that Kevin has stowed in a nice little contraption attached to the head rest and pours us all a glass, before holding his up and saying happily, "To married life and lots of baby making."

We take a sip and I don't miss the way Polly shares a look with Miles and note that she doesn't even take a sip of her own drink.

"Wait just one minute."

I stare at her in shock and she nods, her eyes brimming with unshed tears, "Polly, really, when?"

Freddie looks confused. "Have I missed something?"

Miles looks so proud as he pulls his wife close to his side and says softly, "Polly and I are going to be proud parents in just over six months' time. You are the first to know."

Freddie looks so happy it brings a lump to my throat as the brothers share a moment that I wouldn't have missed seeing for the world. They may have had their problems in the past, but that was a lifetime ago because now they have made it and family matters more than anything. It does to this family and I know they will always be close and it's more than perfect that Polly and I have made the step from best friends forever to sisters. We have all found our happy ever after and what can be better than that?

As the sun sets and we reach Lake View House, the door opens and as we see our family and friends waiting with joyful expressions, it feels more like home than ever. Freddie and I may have relocated a day's journey away, but it's definite our bedrooms will never be empty. Our family and friends will be constant visitors and we may even set up a rival business to Happy Ever After in the future and provide bed-and-breakfast accommodation, but not yet. Now it's just us and a future so exciting, I have to pinch myself to know it's real.

I laugh as I see the familiar faces waiting. The fossil gang, Eloise and Greg, not to mention Sandra, Lizzie and the Major. Alex and Donna made it work and are very welcome guests, along with Kimberly and her new boyfriend, the manager of the Frog and Lily. Lolita Sharples is also there, mingling with Freddie's family, along with my own. Luckily, Freddie's parents are as amazing as he is and his sister has become a firm friend. I couldn't wish for more, but as Freddie and I stand before them all in a group photo, I know that he is worth more than everything rolled into one.

Freddie and I got our happy ever after and the happy ending it guaranteed and now it's up to us to make it count.

The End

THE LAST WORD

I could have carried on writing this story because I fell in love with every last character in this book. This story is very personal to me because 26 years ago, on December 5th 1993, my boyfriend at the time took me out on a date. We went to a teddy bear fair in Brighton because I used to make them as a hobby, and then we went for a roast dinner. I was a little irritated when he then took me for a drive to Dorset! Two hours away and he kept on telling me not to be annoyed and relax.

We parked at the foot of the hill leading to Saint Catherine's Chapel and I think I could barely speak because the last thing I wanted to do was climb a hill in the middle of nowhere on a cold December day. There are walks in Sussex, so who in their right mind drives for two hours to take a walk? You will now realise that I am very slow on the uptake and just stood shivering outside Saint Catherine's Chapel, surrounded by sheep, wondering how much longer before we could head down the hill to the little tea rooms we parked beside.

Then he stood before me, not on one knee I might add,

and asked me to marry him. I was in shock and yet the answer was always yes. We didn't know about the legend of Saint Catherine at the time, although that makes it even more romantic now. It was just a place he had always loved from childhood and wanted it to be special and it was special - it still is.

We have returned many times with our family, our dogs and our daughter. We have stayed in the village and made many memories there. This year we are returning to celebrate our silver wedding anniversary and are staying in a barn with some friends at the foot of the hill. Many of our memories are tied up with Saint Catherine's Chapel, and I know we are not alone. It is a very special place and I hope will always stand as a reminder that happy ever afters are possible, whatever generation you're in.

Thank you for reading Escape to Happy Ever After.

If you liked it, I would love if you could leave me a review, as I must do all my own advertising.

This is the best way to encourage new readers and I

appreciate every review I can get. Please also recommend it to your friends as word of mouth is the best form of advertising. It won't take longer than two minutes of your time, as you only need write one sentence if you want to.

♥

Have you checked out my website? Subscribe to keep updated with any offers or new releases.

When you visit my website, you may be surprised because I don't just write Romantic comedy.

I also write under the pen names M J Hardy & Harper Adams. I send out a monthly newsletter with details of all my releases and any special offers but aside from that, you don't hear from me very often.

I do however love to give you something in return for your interest which ranges from free printables to bonus content. If you like social media please follow me on mine where I am a lot more active and will always answer you if you reach out to me.

Why not take a look and see for yourself and read Lily's Lockdown, a little scene I wrote to remember the madness when the world stopped and took a deep breath?

sjcrabb.com

If you want to know Miles and Polly's story, check out My Christmas Romance.

If you are wondering why Kevin is so strange and want to discover how Lizzie met the Major, all is revealed in My Christmas Boyfriend.

THE LAST WORD

A Festive, Feel Good, Christmas Romance

My Christmas Boyfriend

S J Crabb

MORE BOOKS

The Diary of Madison Brown
My Perfect Life at Cornish Cottage
My Christmas Boyfriend
Jetsetters
More from Life
A Special Kind of Advent
Fooling in love
Will You
Holly Island
Aunt Daisy's Letter
The Wedding at the Castle of Dreams
My Christmas Romance
Escape to Happy Ever After

sjcrabb.com

KEEP IN TOUCH

You can also follow me on the Social media below. Just click on them and follow me.

Facebook

Instagram

Twitter

Website

Bookbub

Amazon

Printed in Great Britain
by Amazon